SILENCE OF STONE

ANNAMARIE BECKEL

SILENCE OF STONE

a novel of Marguerite de Roberval

BREAKWATER BOOKS LIMITED

JESPERSON PUBLISHING • BREAKWATER DISTRIBUTORS

BREAKWATER BOOKS LIMITED

JESPERSON PUBLISHING • BREAKWATER DISTRIBUTORS

100 Water Street • P.O. Box 2188 • St. John's • NL • A1C 6E6
www.breakwaterbooks.com   www.jespersonpublishing.ca

Library and Archives Canada Cataloguing in Publication

Beckel, Annamarie, 1951-

Silence of stone : a novel of Marguerite de Roberval / Annamarie Beckel.

Includes bibliographical references.

ISBN 978-1-55081-243-5

1. Roberval, Marguerite de--Fiction. I. Title.

PS8553.E29552S53 2008   813'.54   C2008-900107-9

Copyright © 2008 Annamarie Beckel

The Canada Council Le Conseil des Arts
for the Arts   du Canada

We acknowledge the financial support of The Canada
Council for the Arts for our publishing activities.

We acknowledge the support of the Department of
Tourism, Culture and Recreation for our publishing
activities.

Canadä

We acknowledge the financial support of the
Government of Canada through the Book Publishing
Industry Development Program (BPIDP) for our
publishing activities.

Printed in Canada

Dedicated to the memory of
Marguerite de Roberval
and to
Elizabeth Boyer whose diligent research
authenticated the documents surrounding
the legend of Marguerite.

"After the first voyage made by Jacques Cartier, as the great king François was desirous, both of learning much, and of hearing about all that was rare and exquisite of foreign lands, he ordered Roberval, a French gentleman, to go to this country of New-Land and from there to go into the land of Canada proper with a good company, and (if he could) to populate this country with native Frenchmen..."

A Collection of Documents Relating to Jacques Cartier and the Sieur de Roberval, as translated by H. P. Biggar, 1930.

"[S]he arrived in France after living for two years and five months in that same place and having come to the village of Nautron [Nontron] country of Perigord, at which time I was with her and she made ample discourse with me of this misadventure and of all her past fortunes."

André Thevet, 1586, *Grande Insulaire*, as translated by Elizabeth Boyer in *A Colony of One*, 1983.

"[H]er Servant, Damienne a native of Normandy, who was an old bawd, aged sixty years who served as protectress of her whom she shielded to play the wanton..."

André Thevet, 1586, *Grande Insulaire*, as translated by Elizabeth Boyer in *A Colony of One*, 1983.

I have made a vocation of forgetting. I work at snuffing memories, one by one. *Sisst, sisst.* Wet fingertips to flame.

Yet, when I am at my work the voices intrude, rekindling hot white fire from grey ash: *Grievous sin. Impardonnable. N'oubliez pas, do not forget.* They torment me with psalms: *How long, O Lord, wilt thou forget me? Out of the depths I have cried to thee.*

I cover my ears, but I cannot silence them.

I heard them first on the island. Soft sibilant whispers, they appeared like a sorcerer's silks pulled from sky, stone, and sea: sapphire, ruby, emerald, ivory. Some were cloaked in ebony feathers. The voices taunted and mocked, comforted and soothed: *Abandoned. Punished. Roberval. Her sin, not yours. L'amour.*

I was on the Isle of Demons for twenty-seven months. Nearly a year alone: three hundred and twenty days. I know, because I kept a careful count: lines scratched on smoke-darkened walls. I hear it yet, the scrape of stone upon stone.

Nonetheless, if you dared to ask, and I deigned to answer, I would tell you that it was not me, but a different Marguerite, who was left on the island. I would tell you that it was she who suffered there, and died.

I would tell you that my life began when I buried her.

I was just twenty-one when Breton fishermen took me from the island and brought me back to France in 1544. I am thirty-seven now. Sixteen years. Yet I continue to dress in black crepe, in widow's weeds, and my hair, unloosed from its widow's cap, falls in long chestnut curls, errant strands of white woven within. My face is indelibly bronzed, and my eyes, once the colour of new spring pastures, have faded to the flat hue of a placid sea – despite what roils beneath. My arms and legs have remained lean and sinewy, and no matter how hard I scrub, the skin of my palms recalls the musky feral scent of a wolf.

I live alone in Nontron, in a small garret above the scrivener's shop. I prefer solitude now, and silence. Low and raspy, my voice is unpleasant, even to me, as if I had swallowed the island's rocks and they lodged in my throat. For too long I had no need to coax words along that stony path, and now I speak as few as I can – and listen to even fewer. The cacophony of voices, their tangled commingling, is too loud and confusing. I cannot discern which words come from without – and which from within.

I am a teacher of little girls. Men of means send their daughters to the school downstairs for lessons in etiquette and elocution. The fathers reveal a certain wariness in the tilt of their heads and the set of their mouths, but they do not forget that Marguerite was a Roberval, that she once danced the *pavane* and *galliard* at the court of King François I. They know that I am the only woman in Nontron who can read and write in both French and Latin, and the fathers want their daughters to be able to read the scriptures, for they have turned away from the Roman Church and embraced the new religion. They are Huguenots.

So I teach the little girls French and Latin, forbidding them their Angoulême dialect, but mostly I teach them to be silent or, if they must speak, to say their words softly so as not to offend my ears. I also teach them needlework, and I teach them numbers and letters, and instruct them in religion. I teach them about the nature of God.

God is not the Word. God is silence.

Roberval. L'amour. Debts must be paid. Silky lapis whispers, echoing as if my narrow room were fifty fathoms across and the walls steep cliffs instead of oak boards.

I sit, staring into the cold hearth. The Franciscan's

questions have rekindled images and memories I believed extinguished long ago. This morning while I was teaching, the monk arrived at the scrivener's door. He read to me the order from the king, dated the twenty-fifth day of March in the year of Our Lord 1560. The order states that Marguerite de la Roque de Roberval is to meet with André Thevet, cosmographer for King François II, each day for a fortnight, the sabbath and saints' days excepted, to tell him all that she knows about Terre Nova, Canada, and New France.

I corrected his Latin. Terra, I said, Terra Nova. And then told him I was not the Marguerite he wanted.

My words carried no meaning for André Thevet, and I have little choice but to obey the king's order. The Franciscan has agreed to meet with me late in the day so I can spend the mornings in the school downstairs.

I taught the girls this morning. They practised forming letters, their chubby fingers clutching thick chunks of chalk, laboriously drawing wobbly lines on roof-slates. Heads bowed, they worked in silence. All except Isabelle. She made bold strokes, her letters a simple task she finished quickly. She placed herself near me then and chattered, lisping through the gap in her front teeth. Her lips are rosy pink and well-defined against creamy skin, and the new teeth coming in look monstrous in her small mouth.

Isabelle is the youngest student. She has been at the school for only a month. When her father first made inquiries he asked nothing about needlework or etiquette or religion, but he considered carefully my terse answers to his questions about French and Latin, ciphering and reading, as if weighing my responses against the hushed rumours he'd heard. Monsieur Lafrenière studied me as if he might know – or wish to know – Marguerite's secrets.

I accepted Isabelle into the school anyway. She reminds me of Marguerite: the same candid gaze, unruly curls, saucy tilt of the head. Her fingers are often stained with black ink, as if she practises her letters at home, on paper.

Hers is the only name I know.

The voices erupt: *La culpabilité. Grievous sin. Impardonnable.*

I put my hands over my ears but cannot stop the tormenting din or the cascade of images: ice-blue eyes, a finger upon the string of a citre, an ebony feather.

Marguerite was just sixteen, and an orphan, when her older cousin, Jean-François de la Roque, Sieur de Roberval, became her guardian. Her lineage was noble, but her father had been among the poorest of the nobility. Roberval had money. He bought clothes to display Marguerite's beauty: a rose silk gown sewn with pearls and cut low and square to expose her breasts, stiffened petticoats to make the gown's rustling skirts cascade from her narrow waist, black brocade slippers embroidered with gold thread and slashed so that puffs of rose silk peeked through.

She was enchanted by the handsome Roberval and even more so by the life he offered. Though a distant cousin, he encouraged Marguerite to call him Uncle. He entertained her with stories about King François, his boyhood friend, and introduced her at court, where even the king's wandering gaze lingered appreciatively upon her. Marguerite curtsied and smiled and kissed a thousand gloved hands.

I touch rough fingertips to my cheeks, then trace my lips and recall plump softness where I now feel only dry parchment.

Grievous sin. Debts must be paid.

"She meant only to save her baby," I answer. "She was punished. She paid."

When Roberval told Marguerite that the king had appointed him Viceroy of New France, she was thrilled and proud to be a Roberval – until he told her that he planned an expedition to Canada and that she would accompany him. In that instant, her pride turned to horror. She'd heard the stories of Canada that circled at court: the wilderness was dreary, cold, and dangerous; Jacques Cartier's men had been attacked and killed by Indians; the explorer Giovanni Verrazzano had been eaten by cannibals. Marguerite could not believe it possible that having only just discovered the pleasures of the court and the delights of her own beauty she would be forced to leave Paris and go to that dreadful wasteland, a frigid land of no cities, no books, no learned conversation. No silks, no pearls, no music. Only monsters and Indians.

The yellow flame of the candle lengthens, too tall and bright for wet fingertips to snuff.

On the sixteenth day of April in 1542, Marguerite –

together with a few noblemen, 16 soldiers, 73 murderers and thieves, seven cows and one bull, eight horses, 35 sheep, 33 goats, and four pigs – stepped aboard the *Vallentyne*.

She saw him at once. Only a few years older than she, he wore a soldier's doublet. His grin startled her. Marguerite returned a coy nod. Though he carried an arquebus, it pleased her to see that his hand cradled a citre, inlaid with ivory and precious metals, far more gracefully than the musket. Michel looked at her and smiled again. His long finger, the nail square and perfect, plucked a single string.

The citre's thrum rings through my head. And through my body. *Le désir.* I close my eyes and my skin remembers. The length of him pressed against her. Fingers fumbling with the lacings of a bodice, the straps of a codpiece. Touch of lips to breast, hand to thighs, her hand on him, the first time she had ever touched a man.

My back arches and I gasp.

The Franciscan hunches forward, hovering like a gluttonous gull over offal. He considers his scattered papers and quills. "What did you use for shelter?" he asks.

Thevet may believe his question innocuous, but it pokes like a sharp beak at my spare flesh.

I clear the gravel from my throat. "She lived at first in a canvas hut."

"She?" He looks at me sideways, one eye squinting.

"Marguerite."

"But you are Marguerite."

"I told you, *Père.* I am not the Marguerite you want."

"Stop being difficult."

I watch his mouth move and hear only the clacking of a yellow beak.

"The king has ordered you to answer my questions." The monk folds his arms over his chest: broad charcoal wings. "Again, what did you use for shelter...Marguerite?"

I hear wind shrieking, claws ripping canvas. "They built huts from the damaged sails Roberval left with them."

"They?"

"Marguerite, her husband, and Damienne, her servant."

"So you will persist in this?" Scowling, he picks up a white quill. "I have heard about this *Damienne.*" His lips pucker as if the name itself tastes sour.

"Damienne was a good woman. She loved Marguerite." I see again her broad smile and round fleshy cheeks, then I blink and see bleeding gums and sharp cheekbones beneath skin as pale and thin as vellum.

"The old bawd. Encouraging such wanton and shameless behaviour...carnal abominations." Thevet takes a sip of wine to wash the foulness from his mouth, then he dips the quill into black ink and begins to scribble.

The king's cosmographer has traveled all the way from Paris to ask his questions. Three hundred miles of rutted muddy roads. Four of the king's soldiers came with the monk to protect him from brigands – and from the zealous adherents of the new religion who abound in Angoulême, so much so that the Catholic chapel in Nontron is little used. We – André Thevet and the one he believes to be Marguerite de Roberval – sit within that chapel, in a small chamber that smells of dank stone and smouldering wood. Faggots hiss and sputter but do not relieve the chill, and the hearth and narrow window offer little light, even in the lengthening days of April.

The Franciscan has lit all four candles on the desk.

He grips the quill so tightly it makes grooves in his fat fingers. "In your desperate state," he says, "did you not accept help from demons?" Thevet softens his eyes, as if he intends sympathy, but their sharp red edges tell me that this is the question that intrigues him most. He taps the nib against the paper: tap-tap-tap.

I turn away and hear in his tapping the raven's *kek-kek-kek*. I nod to acknowledge the warning, but I already know: this man cannot be trusted. I slip my hand within the folds of my skirt to touch the blade of the dagger I carry. It was his dagger, Marguerite's husband's. I trace the dark vein in the mother-of-pearl handle.

The monk awaits my answer, hoping he can call me *hérétique*. But Marguerite was not a heretic. She kept her faith. And I am not a heretic. I am an apostate. I turned my back to God. But not before God turned his back to me.

The Franciscan looks at me with bulbous eyes, yellow-brown marbles in a pasty face. "Aristotle was sceptical that demons exist," he says, "but I have evidence. Mariners have told me that when they passed near the Isle of Demons they heard human voices making a great noise...until they offered prayers and invoked the holy name of Jesus. Then, little by little, the din died away."

The pen quivers above the paper. Thevet wants to hear of hideous forms, lascivious beings who growled and screeched, their breath sulfuric in her nostrils. He believes that Marguerite had to trade away her soul to be rescued from the island. He wants to hear me say it.

"Demons did come to her sometimes," I say cautiously, "mostly when she was alone."

"What did they look like?"

I hear them then, a papery rustling that grows louder: *forty days and forty nights in the wilderness.* An explosion of laughter, then a low growl: *That is nothing, Lord. Nothing.* A long hiss, then ravens' chatter: *quork-quork-quork, pruk-pruk-pruk, km-mm-mm. Eight hundred and thirty-two days, eight hundred and thirty-two nights. Alone for three hundred and twenty, Lord. Would you not accept help from the Devil then?*

"They were black and horrid," I say, "some huge, others small, but always with red eyes."

Not true. There was no Devil but Roberval, no demons. Only the voices: rose, azure, topaz; diaphanous and warm on my shoulders and neck; their breath sweet with cinnamon and cloves. The voices. And the ravens. They have been my companions for more than sixteen years. They are my conversation: taunting, accusing, provoking, comforting. Whispering and wailing, laughing and haranguing, they argue with me and with each other. Neither demon nor angel.

Thevet salivates in anticipation, his lips wet and shiny. "What did they say?" His tongue darts out.

"Nothing. They made only dreadful noises, howling and screeching."

It is easy to lie to the Franciscan. He is credulous, too eager to hear fantastic stories, especially about demons.

"When she prayed, *Père*, or read her New Testament, they went away."

Père. The word grates. I do not believe in his, or God's, paternal affection.

"New Testament!" The monk's doughy face folds easily into another scowl. Now that he can scold, he can hide his trembling eagerness. "Just like a Huguenot, possessing a New Testament, in French," he says. "Reading for yourself, not trusting the Church fathers."

I study the floor to see how one piece of slate is fitted one to the other, no crack wide enough for a wolf's paw or bear's muzzle. Wide enough only for the whispers.

Though the Franciscan is agitated about the new

religion and what he imagines Marguerite believed, he is also careful. Traveling from Paris to Nontron, he has ventured into the stronghold of the Huguenots. And he is not a brave man.

He is also annoyed that he did not learn Marguerite's story years ago from Roberval, whom the monk claims as a great friend. *Mon grand ami*, he has said.

André Thevet huffs like a great white bear, puffed with his own importance and power. In his bluster, he reminds me once again that he is cosmographer for François II and chaplain for the queen-mother, Catherine de Medici. The pompous buffoon is too swelled with himself and his own words to hear anyone else, and I am now certain that I need not divulge Marguerite's secrets, not to an ignorant monk who calls her wanton and shameless, who wishes only to chastise. Thevet would have her play the Magdalene, *la putain repentante*, the penitent whore.

L'idiot. Marguerite's sin had naught to do with her sex.

The candles smoke and drip great pools of stinking tallow. The gorge rises in my throat at the odour of putrid flesh roasting. I look behind the monk's bland face and see a rotting seal wedged in a crevice, eyes hollow, picked by ravens. I smell rancid grease dripping into flames and taste slimy flesh on my tongue.

N'oubliez pas, do not forget. Grievous sin. Impardonnable. Remember, but do not tell. Do not tell.

The voices mingle with the monk's blather about Huguenots. I put my hands to my ears and rock back and forth. "*Non*," I say, "I will not. Stop. Stop."

I look up. Thevet has closed his mouth mid-sentence. I fear at first that he has heard them, but then see that he is merely annoyed, not alarmed. In the sixteen years since the voices first addressed me, I have learned that they speak only for me. No one else ever hears them.

I lower my hands and fold them in my lap. "Please stop," I say quietly. "Do not speak ill of the Huguenots." I do not give a damn about Huguenots, but I assume now a contemplative countenance to make him believe I am considering his most recent aspersions upon Marguerite's faith.

"The demons…tell me more."

"She kept her faith. She prayed. They did not bother her greatly."

He drums his fingers. I wait, knowing that he wants to hear more about demons, but also knowing that he loves his own voice far better than mine. He twirls coarse strands of grey and black beard in pink fingertips, then can restrain himself no longer. He begins lecturing about his journeys through the Levant where, as a young man, he met Turks and Arabs.

"Foolish and superstitious," he proclaims. "I prefer the Tupinamba. Though these wild men of America have no civility at all." He opens his hands wide, the better to share his wisdom. "Walking in darkness and ignorant of the truth, they are not

reasonable creatures. They are subject to many
fantastic illusions and persecutions of wicked
spirits. Indeed, they worship the Devil." The last he
whispers, as if the word itself might seduce him to
heresy. His wine-purpled lips pull to one side.

There is much concern these days about heresy.
The word assumes a twisted black shape above his
head, swirling crepe laced with scarlet ribbons. The
crepe settles like a scapular upon his shoulders, and I
see men and women, throats slit, bellies run through
with sabres, because the Church has called them
heretics. I cannot help wondering what Marguerite,
the believer, would think of a God who ordains such
killing as good. Could she embroider such murder
and torture into a mantle of beauty and grace?

*Give glory to the Lord, for he is good, for his
mercy endureth forever.*

The Franciscan drones on about the Tupinambas'
worship of idols. He has forgotten me. I am naught
but an audience.

Images appear, unbidden: Bones, fragile, like a
robin's. Shallow rocky crypt. Fingernails scraping,
broken and ragged. Hands and feet blue with cold.

La culpabilité. Grievous sin. Impardonnable.

I hear the whimpering of a baby and clench my
teeth to contain the wails building within.

Thevet remembers me then. He dips his quill into
the pot of ink. "Demons?" he asks. "What did you
tell the Queen of Navarre about demons?"

"Nothing. She did not ask about demons."

Shortly after I returned to France, she summoned me to Paris. The Queen of Navarre, sister of François I, held my calloused brown hand within her own soft palms and looked kindly upon me while others stared rudely, mouths gaping. Wildly curious about my adventure, as she called it, the queen listened intently.

Then she offered advice. Roberval is wicked, she said, but not criminal. Foolishly my brother appointed him viceroy. Roberval is the law in New France.

And my *château*? I asked. My properties?

There is nothing you can do, she said. You must leave it to God to punish him. But I will attend to your support. Because God has saved you.

God has saved you. Leave it to God.

I believed the queen would understand Marguerite's story because she too had lost the man she loved when she was a young woman. She too had lost an infant. But the queen took Marguerite's story and retold it in her own collection of tales, changing everything in the telling. Convinced that Marguerite's story was evidence of God's mercy, the queen told a tale of romance and faith. She chose not to mention Roberval's cruelty. She chose not to consider God's neglect.

The Queen of Navarre was the last one, the only one, I ever told about the Isle of Demons. And for sixteen years I have worked at forgetting – until the king's cosmographer arrived yesterday in Nontron. Thevet, to his great irritation, learned only months ago that Marguerite de Roberval was the heroine of the late queen's tale, and so he has come with his order from the king, his quill and his paper, like pick and shovel, to mine for scurrilous details.

For all his mining, I'll give him nothing but fool's gold.

"The queen had no interest in demons. She was far more concerned about the behaviour of Franciscans."

The monk's face flushes, and I smile at his discomfort. Sympathetic to the new religion, the queen satirized Franciscan lechery and greed, depicting monks as pigs that can neither hear nor understand.

"Were the Queen of Navarre not already dead," he sputters, "she would be burned." He pinches his fat lower lip, shutting off any further discussion of the late queen's opinions.

"What of the young man?" he asks. "The lover set ashore with you? Who was he?"

"Marguerite's husband."

"By what rites were you married?"

"Their own."

He smoothes the white feather, trying to feign gentleness and concern. "What was his name?"

"You have no need of a name."

"Of course I do if I am to record this history accurately."

"It is enough to know that he died."

Thevet sits back in his chair and pulls at his beard. "Do you not care that the full truth of this story be known?"

"You will write what you will write. People will believe what they will believe. It does not matter."

"But what about the child?"

"Her baby died." Wails gone to whimpers gone to silence.

"Boy or girl?"

"It does not matter."

He sucks his teeth. "Baptised?" he finally asks.

"*Oui.*"

"What did you name the child?"

The monk leans forward and makes a tent with his fingers. *Le bouffon.* Does he believe me simple-minded, that I would blurt the name of the child and give away the father?

"You can tell me everything." His voice is soft, wheedling. "You have nothing to fear from Roberval… now that he's dead."

I look down to hide the shock I cannot disguise. A score of times I have seen his death in my dreams: the startled blue eyes, the gaping scarlet grin, the gurgling flow of blood. But believed that I had only wished it so.

"You did not know?"

"*Non.*"

"Your guardian," he says, watching me closely, "was murdered last winter, throat slit, at the Church of the Innocents in Paris."

Pale blue voices whisper his name: *Roberval, Roberval.* Then laugh out loud: *His mercy endureth forever. Leave it to God.*

I struggle to contain my own mirth. My throat aches with the effort. I am glad that he is dead, and I hope that he suffered. But it is not for fear of Roberval that I choose not to reveal Marguerite's husband's name. *Non.* The voices demand my silence.

"If you were married, as you allege, and if his family is wealthy…" Thevet strokes the quill against his beard, making an annoying rasp.

"His family was as poor as Marguerite's."

"But they lost a son, an heir. And apparently a grandchild. They would want to know."

"Her husband's family believes that he died a soldier, defending the colony from Indians."

"How did he die?"

"Perhaps they would rather believe in their son's courage and bravery," I say, ignoring the monk's question, "and not know of Roberval's foolishness and cruelty."

"Cruelty!" He points the quill at my heart. "You and your lover sinned. You caused a great scandal. Roberval was justified in punishing you."

I feel anger's dark humour gathering within me, bile rising from deep within my belly.

Abandonnée. La justice. Kek-kek-kek.

Thevet lays down the quill to place a new candle in the holder, his plump fingers clumsy with excited self-righteousness. He lights the candle from another, dripping a greasy tallow circle on his list of questions. The Franciscan can be profligate with candles. And with paper. He is an emissary of King François II.

"They have not yet found his assassin. Would you reveal that name?"

I gag at the stink. And the accusation. "Roberval was a cruel leader. There are many who hate him, many who would wish him dead."

"Did you?"

"Did I not have cause?"

"Did you kill him?"

"And how would I have traveled to Paris?"

He shuffles his papers and looks toward the window. "You could have flown," he mumbles.

L'imbécile. I cannot stop the howl that explodes from my throat. I try to quiet my laughter before I speak. "*Père,* if I possessed the powers of a witch, Roberval would have been dead long ago."

Thevet raises a finger as if he has just solved a difficult puzzle. "Ah, but it is safe to kill him now...now that his protectors – François I and Henri – are dead."

I tilt my chin and allow myself a small provocation. "Don't you mean François I and Diane de Poitiers – King Henri's whore? The whore was Roberval's cousin."

"How dare you!" His nostrils flare, and I see pale wiry hairs glistening against ruddy skin. He takes deep breaths to calm himself. "How dare you speak of Henri's trusted advisor in such terms." His face is pinched, as if he has a griping in his bowels. "But then again, you have always lacked propriety. Indulging yourself in carnal abominations."

The yellow clack, clack, clack of his words circles between us: *La convenance. Carnal abominations.*

We sit quietly, watching the words spin, listening to his belly rumble, until Thevet can contain himself no longer. "Did you hire someone?"

I stand, and without waiting for the Franciscan's assent, turn and walk away. I can hear his agitated huff behind me.

Hurrying through the sanctuary, I do not cross myself, nor do I bend a knee to the Christ who was deaf to her prayers. I turn my back to him, draw my cloak and hood around me, and push open the arched door. I step from the chapel into the rain, my foot crushing lily-of-the-valley. I bend low to touch the wounded white bells, to draw within their sweet fragrance and dispel the dank odour of granite, the putrid stink of tallow.

I sit near the hearth, wrapped in a wool blanket. I am always cold. And no matter how much I eat, I am thin and hungry, bone knocking against bone. When the little girls bring biscuits from home, I want to snap them up and swallow them whole. They see my hunger, the copper glint of a wolf's eyes, and hide their biscuits in the folds of their skirts.

The glowing embers wink and yawn puffs of smoky breath: *La meurtrière, murderer. La culpabilité. La justice.*

Did I kill him? Certainly it would have been easy. He was too arrogant to be wary. I'd do it without malice, simply slide a sharp blade across his throat as if he were a fox or a deer, then listen for the gush that quiets to a gurgle, the last hissing breath. I'd leave his body, and his skin. I have no need of either now.

But I made no trip to Paris last winter. Did I? I rub my temples. I forget so much, and my eyes and ears play tricks. The thud of raindrops against the roof becomes the roaring crash of the sea. I hear wind shrieking when oak leaves barely tremble. White bears lurk behind doors, their *huff-huff-huff* punching holes in the dark. I smell the hot meaty breath of wolves and hear their claws clicking on stone. I see iron clouds fall to earth and pewter rain rise into molten sky to blot out the opal moon that floats there, unattached, like *un esprit*, a ghost. I pass whole nights within the embracing arms of maples, beeches, and oaks, listening for the rustle of feathers, the soft beat of ebony wings, and believe I have been there but an hour. The impertinent sun surprises me.

Often I cannot remember teaching the little girls, but no one comes to tell me that I was not downstairs, so I must have been.

I have forgotten much of what happened to Marguerite. But not nearly enough. Would that I could forget all of it. Everything. But the voices do not allow that: *Grievous sin. Impardonnable. La culpabilité.*

And now the Franciscan would have me remember: *Wanton and shameless. La putain, whore.*

I kept her New Testament, faded and yellowed by salt wind and salt tears – tears wasted on unanswered prayers – to remind me of God's indifference.

The voices mock: *Have mercy on me, O Lord, for*

I have cried to thee all the day...Out of the depths I have cried to thee. How long, O Lord? How long?

Her New Testament, Michel's dagger, the iron pot, the black feather: that's all I took from the island. Too little. But more than I want. I sometimes think I should have stayed there, that I should lie beside them, my bones a part of that place.

I pull out the dagger and make a long slit across my wrist. Red beads well.

Non. I forget much, but I would not forget three hundred miles of mud and biting winds nor that final satisfying image: ice-blue eyes filled with white-hot terror.

I did not kill him. But I wish I had.

The Franciscan suspects I may have hired someone. How foolish. I have little money, only the few coins I collect for teaching the girls and the small pension the Queen of Navarre arranged for me. Not nearly enough to hire an assassin. Unless? Unless he hated Roberval as much as I do. He'd do it then for the sheer pleasure of the doing.

Do I know such a man?

I wake, panting, his wrathful eyes boring into me. I feel burning in the centre of my chest. Think. Think. He is dead now. But in the darkness, I see his face, white as alabaster and just as cold and hard. The perfectly sculpted lips curve in a cruel smile.

I light a candle from embers in the hearth. The candles are beeswax, costly, but I cannot abide the stink of tallow. I use them sparingly.

I feel a sharp pain at my wrist. I pull back my bloody sleeve and see a cut, as if a white bear's claw had sliced across my arm. I have no memory of injury.

Debts must be paid. La culpabilité. La pénitence.

"She paid," I answer. "She paid."

I cannot keep my teeth from chattering. I wrap the wool blanket tightly around me. On the island cold crept into my bones and resolutely will not be dislodged.

Twenty-seven months on the Isle of Demons. Roberval never returned. Only two months after he arrived in Canada, he sent two ships back to La Rochelle for more provisions. Little more than a year after he founded his wretched colony at Charlesbourg Royal, those who survived the winter returned to France. The ships must have passed by the island, but not one of them stopped. Not one.

Twenty-seven months. Not a shipwreck, not an accident. Punished. Left to die.

It was only by chance that a ship stopped at the island. The Breton fishermen wanted fresh water. Not Marguerite.

How my arrival back in France must have startled Roberval. Startled, but never worried. He had his position as Viceroy of New France to protect him, as well as his friend, King François I, and his cousin, Diane de Poitiers, King Henri's mistress.

And now he is dead. Murdered at the Church of the Innocents. For sixteen years I have longed for this. But now I know: his death changes nothing.

God's little irony.

I put my hands to my cheeks and allow myself a small memory: ivory skin, bold lips, eyes the colour of new grass. Marguerite had no memory of her mother's face, not even a portrait, for her mother had died when she was born. With grave sorrow pulling down his words, Marguerite's father told her that she resembled her mother, that she was beautiful in the same way: wild and wilful, strong-minded and strong-bodied, beguiling but guileless.

Her family owned a small *château* but could afford no servants. Marguerite laboured like a maid of all work: cooking and washing dishes and clothes, spinning and weaving, tending sheep and clipping their wool, growing vegetables, hauling wood and water, milking goats, butchering chickens and pigs, rendering fat and making cheese.

L'orpheline misérable.

"*Non.*" I shake my head. "*Non*, she was not a miserable orphan. She had her father, and he loved her. She was not unhappy."

A man of good intentions and sympathetic to the new religion, Marguerite's father attended to her education himself. Though it was costly, he did not stint on books, paper and quills, or on lamp oil and candles, so that she could read and study during the long dark evenings. He discussed with her ideas about philosophy and religion, entrusting to her an expensive copy of the New Testament.

I brush my fingers across the tooled leather cover, lift the pages with my thumb, and listen as they flutter closed again, whispering God's secrets.

Once I nearly boiled the cover for broth.

Marguerite learned psalms and prayers, singing them in both Latin and French. Her father, fostering in her a piety well beyond her years, helped to create in Marguerite a fractious alliance of scepticism and devotion, obstinacy and obedience, pragmatism and romance: a young girl at war with herself, headstrong and heartstrong.

La tête forte. Le cœur fort. But not strong enough for the island. Être indulgent, c'est mourir.

"*Oui,*" I say. "To be soft is to die."

When she was just sixteen, her father died suddenly, of no cause a country doctor could discern, though neighbours whispered that he had died of a grief he could no longer bear. Roberval became Marguerite's guardian. He dressed elegantly, and Marguerite was ashamed at first of her peasant roughness and poverty. But Roberval disdained neither her clothes nor her calloused hands and ragged nails. Instead he bought creamy silk gloves to cover her hands until they softened, until the nails grew smooth and oval from disuse.

Roberval hired a servant for Marguerite, an older widow from Normandy. Damienne was plump and cheerful and garrulous, and she delighted in her charge: *une belle demoiselle* whom she could dress like a doll and fuss and fret over. Never having known a mother, Marguerite came to love Damienne's chatter and her solicitous ministrations.

When Roberval began consulting Marguerite about his business ventures and investments, as if he esteemed her opinion, as if he valued her education, especially her knowledge of Latin, she revelled in his attentions.

La vanité. La fille naïve. La coquette.

I hear their contempt. Despite the smouldering fire, I breathe in the arid essence of silk and taffeta and books. The fragrance of wet earth and new grass drifts in through the open window. The fresh scent growing from winter's decay brings a shudder. April. The season when Roberval's ships left La Rochelle for New France.

I burrow deeper into my blanket and stare into the small flame, the remembering unbearable now, far, far worse than the cut on my wrist.

I will myself to sleep, to forget.

I feel a presence, a soul nearby. I look up and see iridescent green eyes staring at me through the open window. A striped face, a tattered ear. I creep toward the window, but the cat is wary. It turns and flees, agile despite a stiff back leg that gives it a bouncing gait, like a pirate with a wooden leg.

I go to the drawer for a leather cord, stretch it out to its full length, then twist and tie a knot. I set the snare in the narrow space between my garret and the next. If I had a bit of meat or cheese, I would lay bait. The cat is thin and rangy. Still, I am hungry. I am always hungry.

The girls are practising embroidery, their fingers clumsy. My own eyes are gritty from passing thread through the eyes of their needles, over and over again. I keep my sleeve pulled down to cover my wrist.

The girls bend their heads over their hoops. All except Isabelle. She is plaiting a scarlet thread into her dark hair. "Madame de Roberval," she says, "look at me. *Je suis belle, non?*"

"Your father does not pay for you to play. How can you help your mother if you do not learn to work?"

Her grin disappears. "Mama is dead."

"All the more reason to work hard." I pick up her hoop and turn it over. The back of the cloth is a welter of tangles and knots.

Isabelle pouts. "I hate embroidery. My fingers are poked full of holes."

"We must often do what is hateful to us." I look at my hands. Instead of smooth ovals, I see nails ragged and bleeding from scraping for mussels. Dry bones. A dead gull, flesh gone. Sucking on the tips of white feathers, my belly cavernous and hollow. My hands and feet are suddenly numb with cold.

Isabelle gives a saucy flick of her curls, then begins to remove the red thread, perhaps glad the day is nearly at an end and there will be no more embroidery for her today. Yet she lingers after the other girls are gone. She steps close, touches her fingertips to my hand, and offers a tentative contrite smile.

My lips cannot soften to return it.

Isabelle turns and runs out the door. I hear her happy exclamation: "Papa!" And imagine Monsieur Lafrenière in his black doublet and plain white cuffs. Unlike the other fathers, he wears no rings, no jewels on his cap, no family crest on his chest.

Yet Isabelle has paper, quills, and ink.

Opposite the window a small square of ochre light moves slowly across the wall. I watch how the stones wrinkle the light.

The Franciscan shuffles papers, pretending that he has no need to apologize for his ludicrous accusation that I hired someone to kill Roberval. He is the cosmographer for King François II, the chaplain for Catherine de' Medici. He will apologize for nothing.

My wool sleeve catches on the wound at my wrist. The cut itches.

Thevet sighs. "It is to be regretted that Roberval's colony failed. It would have brought the king immortal honour – and the grace of God – to have rescued these barbarous people from ignorance and brought them to the Church."

He leans forward, his face a mask of concern. "Tell

me everything," he says quietly, as if we were conspir-
ators. "Start at the beginning. Tell me about Canada."

There is a long silence while I try to compose an
answer. Thevet toys with his quills, trying not to
show his impatience. He cannot wait long. "That
great mariner, Jacques Cartier, is one of my best
friends," he says. "He has told me much."

I suspect the monk is lying. Cartier was
discerning, determined, and to the young Marguerite,
handsome and courageous. Never would such a man
be a great friend to the imbecile who sits before me.

I am content to listen to the guttering candles,
but Thevet rushes to fill the quiet. "The Hochelaga
Indians are the ones best known to the French.
Indeed, Cartier brought two of them to the king.
In their religion they have no other method or
ceremony of worshipping or praying to their god
than to contemplate the new moon."

I stare into the ochre light and see a tall man
standing amidst fog. He is dressed in hides, his sleek
hair pulled up in a knot. Tethered to the knot, and the
same colour as his hair, an ebony feather turns in the
wind and brushes his cheek. I hear a feather's rasp,
but it is only the monk smoothing his quill.

Thevet burbles on, "The Indians were well treat-
ed by the French." He raises a finger for emphasis.
"And for this very reason they claimed that their god,
who had told them the bearded foreigners had killed
their men, was a liar."

Whose god is a liar? I shout in my head.

"Marguerite was obedient," I say out loud. "She

went with her uncle. But she learned nothing of Canada. She knew only the Isle of Demons."

He does not hear my bitterness.

When Roberval insisted that Marguerite and Damienne go with him to New France, Damienne put her hands to her face, her mouth and eyes a triangle of round O's. Ships disappear, she worried aloud, never to be seen again. Dragons and monsters abound in those lands, *les sauvages*.

Marguerite was terrified. She protested and argued, wept and pleaded, but Roberval was adamant.

For how long? she asked.

Roberval would give her no answer, saying only that he would make his fortune in New France.

But how long? Marguerite persisted. A year? Two? Five? A lifetime?

"You seem to forget, Marguerite, that it was your own scandalous behaviour that placed you on the Isle of Demons," the monk says, "and by God's grace that you survived. Quite miraculously, I would say."

Laughter flows from the stones: *How long, O Lord? How long wilt thou forget me? How long wilt thou turn thy face from me? Km-mm-mm. Saved by our grace, not God's.*

"Marguerite obeyed," I repeat, shutting out the voices, "but she missed the…" I search for a word. "Amenities of the court."

"Ah, a spoiled coquette even then."

"*Non*, Marguerite was not a coquette. She craved learned conversation, talk of books and ideas."

"Books and ideas?" Thevet scoffs. "The Queen of Navarre poisoned you, and many others, with talk of new ideas, talk of the new religion. Thanks be to God that King Henri dealt firmly with all of that."

All of that. The Franciscan blathers on about heretics, as if *all of that* is of little consequence. An inconvenience. Men hanging from the ramparts at Amboise. Burnings. *La Chambre Ardente*, King Henri's Burning Chamber. All for a God who does not hear them, a God who does not answer.

How long, O Lord? How long? My bones are grown dry.

Marguerite prayed that her uncle would change his mind. When he did not, she screwed up her courage, because she believed that her uncle loved her, that he insisted on her accompanying him to Canada because he could not bear to be so long without her.

Jacques Cartier, her uncle's second-in-command, set sail from La Rochelle in May 1541, but Roberval was forced to delay his departure. He could find no one willing to go with him. Men would go to Terre Neuve to fish – but they wanted to return again to France when the season ended.

Marguerite felt reprieved, as if God, at long last, had listened and intervened. She hoped desperately, and prayed with renewed fervour, that Roberval would choose not to go at all.

Finally, after a year's delay, King François agreed to release two hundred felons from prison, upon pain of death if they returned to France. Roberval, using all his considerable charm, succeeded in persuading a dozen impoverished noblemen to venture forth, promising they would make their fortunes in New France.

On the sixteenth day of April in 1542, Marguerite and a trembling Damienne, together with noblemen and soldiers and the freed murderers and thieves, boarded the *Vallentyne*, the *Sainte-Anne*, and the *Lèchefraye*.

The Franciscan is finished with heretics for now. "Did you know him before you left France?" he asks. "Or did you meet him aboard ship?"

"Who?"

"Your lover," he says impatiently.

"She did not know him in France. He boarded the *Vallentyne* with her...before the murderers and thieves." I see their sallow pockmarked faces, sneers filled with dark stubby teeth and bleeding gums. But I can also see Michel's mischievous grin and the gold flecks in his eyes that promised love.

"A nobleman?"

"*Oui.*"

"What happened on the voyage to anger Roberval?"

I shrug a shoulder against my neck. "They courted." Dark beard tickling her skin, fingers dancing across the tops of her breasts. Her mouth on his, tongues exploring.

"Your uncle would not have objected to mere courting. Obviously there was more," he insists. "There was sin, Marguerite, grievous sin...for which you must beg God's forgiveness." Thevet's lip curls as if he is disgusted by the thought of bodies and desire.

Spit gathers in my mouth. I would send it flying onto his curled lip if I could. Marguerite sinned, but not with Michel. They merely loved. As if one can love, merely.

"Marguerite paid dearly for her sins."

Thevet does not hear. He stands and points at me, as if to emphasize the importance of his suppositions. "Perhaps you believed yourself to be a savage. Among the savages, girls are not scorned for having *served* young men before they are married." His tongue flicks out and lingers at the corner of his mouth, and I know that he only pretends at his disgust for desire.

"I understand from Cartier that there are even certain lodges where they meet, the men *to know* the women." He smoothes his cassock, his hand hovering over his crotch. He watches to see if I am looking.

I turn away and try to forget what he has made me see. I hear worms in the graveyard outside, gnawing at the newly dead.

"They were married," I say.

He snorts. "A hand-fast marriage…a marriage for peasants, not nobles."

The Franciscan sits down and riffles through his notes. "Roberval's records are incomplete. Pages are missing. But it appears there were only seven noblemen aboard the *Vallentyne*: Roberval himself, La Salle, de Velleneuve, La Brosse, de Longueval, de Mire, de Lespinay." He lifts an eyebrow. "Which one did you choose for your sin?"

"Their love was not a sin."

"*Putain!* Even now you would show no contrition?" His bulbous eyes bulge even more. "Roberval was right to punish you."

"He could have married them," I say quietly. "They would have been the first married couple in his colony."

"But you and your lover had sinned. Roberval had to set an example to the other colonists."

"To murderers and thieves?"

"Precisely. There was an obvious need for Roberval's strict discipline."

I hear the leather biting into flesh, and the screams. I see flayed backs. A man dangles from the yardarm, legs kicking, then still. The stink of his bowels fills the room.

I rub my wounded wrist. "Roberval had no need to set an example. He wanted Marguerite to die."

Thevet flinches. "Preposterous! *Non*, it was with terrible sadness that he punished you. He told me so himself."

I laugh out loud, unable to reconcile the ice-blue eyes with sorrow. "Why do you think, *Père*, that all records of Marguerite have vanished?"

His hands flutter. "Records are often incomplete, pages missing."

My voice is weary of talking, and I am weary of Thevet. I have said far too much already, but I must say one thing more. "It was Roberval who destroyed the records."

"To what end?"

"To hide the identity of Marguerite's husband."

"Why would he do that?"

"Because he feared that her husband's family would bring a suit against him."

"But Roberval was viceroy. He was the law."

"They are nobles. They could have brought a petition to King François."

His tawny eyes pull away from me, and I know he is struggling to solve the puzzle. What family in France, he is asking himself, is so powerful they would dare to bring a petition against Roberval to King François?

I offer Thevet these parting words: "None of the men on your list was Marguerite's husband."

The noose dangles empty. The striped cat is shrewd. I re-set the snare, then wrap myself in a blanket and sit near the fire, fingers drumming, drumming, drumming against my thigh. The Franciscan's questions have breathed life into small dusty carcasses that had lain amidst ashes and rotting earth. Words, memories, images buzz like so many dung-covered flies, a humming din in my head: *La belle fille. Innocente. L'amour, le désir. Pearly bones. Dead eye to bloody sky. La culpabilité. Grievous sin. Impardonnable. Km-mm-mm.*

A spider weaves her web among faggots stacked near the hearth. Her legs move gracefully, embroidering one silky strand to another, and I listen for the song as her legs pluck each delicate string – a simple melody, like one of Michel's *chansons*. The spider is ravenous for small creatures, but meticulous and patient in setting her snare, and I decide to release to her the buzzing winged beasts hovering in my head. She will catch them and bind them, then eat them at her leisure, and they will be gone from me.

My first offering is a slender blue damselfly, wings like silver gossamer. "*L'amour*," I say quietly.

La putain. La meurtrière. Murderer. Le sang rouge.

"*L'amour*," I shout out loud to silence the other voices.

In their first few days at sea, Marguerite and Damienne walked about on deck, bored and fretful, wary of the wind and waves. Though familiar with the stink of pigs and chickens, Marguerite now proclaimed the odours offensive, and she walked with a lavender-scented handkerchief pressed to her nose. To keep her hair from tangling in the wind, she confined her chestnut curls within a fine mesh snood sewn with pearls, and she scurried below when she thought the salt wind and sea spray too harsh on her skin. Amused by Marguerite's pretensions, Damienne encouraged them nonetheless, suspecting that a certain young nobleman, who seemed to contrive for his path to cross theirs, might find them charming.

Marguerite had known men who were far more handsome, her uncle among them, but Michel's face, unblemished by pox and with pointed dark beard neatly trimmed, pleased her. His grin, which came easily and often, transformed his somewhat ordinary comeliness into a portrait that made the articulate Marguerite stumble on her words.

He'd trained only briefly as a soldier, and though neither lazy nor profligate, he carefully explained, he had found himself ill-suited to the military life, a life of discipline and obedience. His family, like Marguerite's, was noble but poor.

Michel thumped a fist to his heart. But I will make a new fortune in New France, he proclaimed, Roberval has promised us that. Gold and precious jewels lying upon the ground for the taking, the viceroy says.

But *les sauvages*, Damienne whispered. What about them?

Michel waved a hand, dismissing her concerns. There are many soldiers among us, he said, with guns. The Indians will not be a problem. And when they see what civilization and religion can offer them, they will soon become our allies.

Marguerite seized upon Michel's enthusiasm. He gave her hope that Canada would be neither as dreadful nor as dangerous as she imagined. He became a delightfully pleasant distraction from her fears and worries.

Nevertheless, Marguerite remained mindful of her station as ward of the viceroy, and she tried not to linger overly long in Michel's company. Yet she found herself inexorably drawn to his good cheer and conversation. Though she read her New Testament and prayed daily, and liked to think of her heart as pious and devout, she also recognized within herself a fluttery yearning that could not be denied, a yearning that made her cheeks colour whenever she saw Michel.

Damienne's smile was indulgent. He may be poor, but he is a nobleman, the old widow reasoned. Your uncle did not object to young men's attentions when you were at court. Why would he do so now?

I run my thumb along the sharp blade of the dagger. How naive they had been. Why, indeed, would Roberval object? I place the point in my palm, but resist pushing it through.

Michel, who knew even less about sailing than he did about soldiering, did little work aboard ship. With felons at his disposal, Roberval could hardly assign a nobleman to the galley or to feed the livestock or to dispatch manure and the contents of chamber pots into the sea.

Idle, and perhaps to the viceroy's eyes useless, Michel began coming to their cabin to play his citre for Marguerite and Damienne. He was not a skilled musician, but Marguerite cared little about that. She was enthralled. She danced within the narrow confines of the cramped and airless cabin and imagined herself back at court, lustrous pearls at her throat, colourful silks and taffetas rustling. The music reminded her of the Queen of Narvarre from whom she'd learned about Erasmus and Thomas à Kempis. She and the queen had enjoyed talking long into the night, sometimes singing psalms together. It had been thrilling – this clandestine talk that skirted closely upon heresy – and made Marguerite eager to discuss theology and philosophy with Michel. She was surprised, and just a little chagrined, to find him neither knowledgeable about nor interested in books and ideas.

Erasmus and his ilk are not great men in New France, Michel teased, their philosophies are like ash, dead and useless, far less important than muskets and gold and jewels. Then Michel, his face sculpted anew by his charming smile, would play his citre, and Marguerite had only to close her eyes to smell rose petals and lilies scenting air that stank of chamber pots and manure.

After little more than a fortnight, when Michel met them on deck, Damienne found reasons to retire to the cabin, but not before she'd wagged an admonishing finger at Marguerite. I will give you privacy, she warned, but do not forget *la chasteté et la virginité*. Do not ever think of yourselves as alone. Always there is someone watching.

Michel manoeuvred then to stand too close, to touch Marguerite's forearm or hand, to brush his lips against her cheek. She discouraged him, but without conviction.

Vous êtes belle, he said.

Tu, she corrected, *tu*.

She never intended to love. But she did – perhaps loving the comfort and distraction Michel offered as much as the alluring young man himself. Caught up in each other, Marguerite and Michel were oblivious, unmindful of watching eyes and wagging tongues, and foolish enough to believe that the darkness was deep enough to cover them, that the sly eye of the moon would not reveal them.

Je t'adore, Michel told her, his breath warm on her neck as his fingers trailed across the tops of her breasts then inched beneath her skirts. I love you above all else, he said. We will marry and make our fortune together in New France.

Her throat closed. Marry? Did she want to marry? But she could not think upon that just then, not with her spine and thighs softening against him. She nearly cried out with the agonizing desire his caresses provoked. Later, within the confines of the cabin, in the terrible solitude of her narrow bunk, she writhed, entangling herself in the bedclothes. She would have touched herself were it not such a grievous sin.

Desire battled with piety and chastity. Piety and chastity won. Briefly.

The spider's slender thread vibrates, a high-pitched ringing: the blue damselfly caught, twisting. Laughter, like rose silk rustling: *La piété et la chasteté. La demoiselle naïve. Le désir.*

Unfastening the black cap from my head, I let my hair fall loose. I slip a hand inside my chemise and touch a breast, close my eyes and remember.

I do not care about sin.

The girls are doing sums. I have not yet taught them that their lives will be subtraction, not addition.

A small hand touches mine. *"J'ai fini!"* It is Isabelle, always finished before the others. She holds out her slate, her small chin jutting. Isabelle's skin is like satin, like a baby's. Her lips are full and pink. Lips like Michel's. I long to trace them with a finger.

I pull my hand away from hers and do not bother to check her slate. I know already that her sums are correct.

"Madame de Roberval," she says, "can you teach me to write poetry?"

"You are too young for poetry."

"Papa thinks I am ready."

Poetry. Marguerite had read hundreds of poems. She could recite lines from dozens: psalms, but also frilly exclamations of love, rapturous stanzas extolling golden tresses and ivory breasts, lyric lines praising the frail beauty of blooms confined in rock-walled gardens, barren refrains proclaiming God's grace and mercy.

Marguerite loved poetry. I am contemptuous of it all.

"Let your papa teach you poetry," I say.

"Papa says he is a geographer and an alchemist, not a poet. He says that all well-bred ladies know how to write poetry…that you must know how and that I should learn from you."

I consider her open face, the smooth forehead and clear eyes. Isabelle can hide nothing, but I wonder about her father. What is Monsieur Lafrenière hiding? What does he know of Marguerite? What does he know of me?

"Papa never tells me I am too young. For anything. He lets me stand on a stool by his bench and watch him mix elix…" Isabelle chatters through her missing teeth, lisping the s's. The smooth forehead creases now as she searches for the word she cannot quite remember.

She taps an ink-stained finger against her cheek. "Thingth," she says at last. "He does not let me stir them yet, but he will soon. And Papa lets me look at maps and read whatever I choose, so long as I wash my hands and do not crease the pages."

"Your papa is good to you."

I walk to the window and grip the sill. A geographer, an alchemist who toys with dark secrets. What does Monsieur Lafrenière want to know? Would he take Marguerite's story and transmute lead into gold?

Isabelle trails behind and pulls at my skirt. "Will you teach me? Please?" She holds out her slate. She has already rubbed out her sums and written four uneven lines: *Mama est au paridis / Elle aime Papa et Isabelle / Elle attend Papa et Isabelle / Mama est au paridis.*

I did not tell Isabelle that no one awaits our arrival in heaven, that love is long dead before the clods of earth rain down upon the coffin, before the stones are rolled into place. Instead I corrected her spelling. "*A*," I said, pointing to her slate, "*au paradis.*" Then I searched and found a volume of poetry for her to study: vacuous verses about love, invoking mountains and sea and sky, as if love and nature were sweetness and beauty and joy, as if love continued beyond the grave.

I sit in the empty classroom, reluctant to go to the chapel. The slender volume of poetry lies open before me, but I cannot bring myself to read a single word.

I dreamed last night of walking in the woods, of listening for ebony wings and watching for wolves' copper eyes, and for bears, white shadows looming in the dark. I dreamed last night of Roberval and of Michel. I followed a trail of grey rock, footprints in snow and ice. This morning my slippers were damp.

Naively enthusiastic and desperate with desire, Marguerite went to Damienne. She cast her gaze to the floor, then she begged, Can you leave us alone in the cabin?

Non, non, Damienne answered, shaking her head so vigorously the loose flesh beneath her chin wobbled. *La chasteté. La virginité.*

We are to be married, Marguerite answered. When we arrive in Terre Neuve, I will ask my uncle, and he will marry us...on land, not at sea.

Then you must wait.

We cannot.

But you must.

If we cannot be in the cabin, Marguerite insisted,

desire making her bold, we will make love on deck, for all to see.

But you cannot!

We will.

Damienne bit her lip. You are quite certain you and he will be married, that you can trust this man?

Oui. Marguerite stamped a foot.

Michel crept into the cabin, a shy nod to Damienne. With a disapproving scowl, she withdrew, and the young lovers hesitated only briefly. They fulfilled their desire with abandon, their coupling less artful than ardent. Stealth and restraint had only added to their passion. For Marguerite, there was pain and blood, but she was desperate to touch and caress, desperate with the longing for a consummation only *une demoiselle naïve* could imagine.

Sniffing the back of my wrist, I remember the smell of his skin, salt and berries, the feel of his hands on her breasts and hips. Memory of strong legs entangled with hers, his movement within, filling the hungry longing between her thighs.

And then the other. A small white scar, mahogany eyes. An ebony feather twisting in the wind, soft rasp against brown cheek.

I close the book of poetry and force myself to stand and walk to the window. I can see almost nothing through circles of translucent glass the colour of the sea. I consider the swirls, so like waves, and tap at the small bubbles trapped within. I smell salt and hear the hull of a ship creaking. I smell love.

Marguerite and Michel loved, and imagined their

loving to be secret. Reluctantly Damienne agreed to act as their sentinel, patiently holding vigil and frowning her disapproval. Marguerite still met with Roberval to discuss with him his plans for New France, but she now watched him closely for any sign that he knew.

Le scandale. Roberval. Le cœur noir.

"*Oui,*" I say, my finger tracing the dark lead between the circles of glass. "A black heart."

The three ships arrived in St. John's on the eighth day of June, slipping past the high cliffs and through the narrow opening to the harbour. Marguerite counted seventeen other vessels, mostly French and Portuguese. Ramshackle sheds huddled near the water, and long wharves reached out like bent and twisted fingers.

Thick slabs of fish dried beneath the bright sun and brisk wind, which was redolent with the stink of offal. Flies formed humming black clouds above the fish and competed with screeching gulls for refuse. Nonetheless, to the would-be colonists the smells of St. John's were a welcome relief from the stench of the ships, from the foul miasma created by livestock and the filth of their own bodies. They were glad for the chance to drink sweet water and wine that did not taste like vinegar, grateful for a bite of fresh meat and a mouthful of something crisp and green. They were eager to disembark and walk upon dry land that did not roll and sway beneath their feet.

Roberval was careful at first about whom he allowed to go ashore, but he soon realized there was no place for his felons to hide, nowhere he could not track them down again. They could escape into the hills and woods away from the small settlement, but that would be a fate worse than the colony in New France. Roberval was also satisfied that he'd succeeded in instilling fear and loathing within the colonists. His punishments had been harsh: flogging just for stealing an extra bit of hard bread, hanging for disobeying an order, any order. Harsh, but necessary. None of his men would dare to try to escape.

Roberval. Le cœur noir.

I blink and shake my head, but cannot stop the visions of bloodied backs, of a body swinging with the waves until the flesh turned black. I grip the windowsill and stare into the swirls of green glass until I can replace those images with grasses and white daisies bending with the wind.

While in St. John's, Roberval took on supplies of fresh water, salt fish, and whatever fresh meat and vegetables he could confiscate, taking whatever he wanted by force. Recognized by the French as viceroy, and relishing that authority, he spent his days settling disputes between sailing captains and fishermen, between French and Portuguese, the latter protesting loudly that Roberval had no command over them.

Eventually Roberval permitted nearly everyone to go ashore, even Michel and Marguerite, who had lived in terrible fear that Roberval had found them out, that he would now put them on separate ships. He seemed not to know, however, and Marguerite felt encouraged by his lack of attention. Nevertheless,

Marguerite and Michel were careful to leave the *Vallentyne* separately.

Later, in their wanderings together, they discovered a small meadow where they could lie beneath the sun's golden eye, the tall grasses blowing in slow waves around them, the sound like rustling satin. White daisies bloomed in abundance, and Marguerite inhaled deeply, the clean fragrance of grasses and daisies a welcome relief from the fetid odours aboard the *Vallentyne*. Even the salt air smelled sweeter here.

Marguerite and Michel bathed in an icy stream, then made love slowly, their bodies still wet and glistening.

This is what it will be like in New France, Michel said, we will love under the blue, blue sky on a bed of grasses and flowers. His eyes became soft and dreamy. And we will order books from France, and you will teach our children to read and to write. You will teach them to cipher.

He stroked her smooth belly then kissed it. The touch of his beard tickled, and Marguerite laughed. Our many, many children, he whispered into her belly, his breath warm.

Michel urged caution in approaching Roberval about the question of marriage, perhaps understanding his nature far better than Marguerite did. With prodding from an insistent Damienne, however, Marguerite finally gathered her courage and went to her uncle. She carefully listed Michel's merits and her own dowry, and then told Roberval that she and Michel wanted to marry.

Would you, as viceroy, perform the ceremony?

Non, he said. I will not.

Marguerite was stunned. But we are well-suited, she said, and I love him. And he loves me.

Roberval's lips curved into a tight smile. Love has nothing to do with marriage, he said.

But who else is there? Who?

You will *not* marry him.

I will, Uncle. I will!

Roberval drew back his arm and slapped her, so hard that she fell to her knees. Foolish girl, he said. Without my permission your union cannot be legal. You will marry no one.

I put a hand to my cheek and feel the stinging burn, the humiliation purple like a bruise, streaked with yellow confusion and black anger.

Marguerite scrambled to her feet. Before she could unlatch the door and flee, he said, You have already lain with him, haven't you? *La putain!* Whore!

Lain with Michel. La putain! Whore! Le scandale.

The voices are like cobwebs covering my hair and face. I wave my hands to brush them away.

Michel saw her running and followed her to the cabin. When Marguerite told him what had happened, he put a trembling palm to either side of her face, careful not to touch her swelling cheek. I will kill him, he said.

Non, non! Then you will be killed, hanged as a traitor.

But this...*this*. How could he do this to you?

He is viceroy.

Why would he forbid you to marry?

I do not know, she said. She considered, then discarded the other noblemen on the expedition. Surely Roberval did not intend for her to marry one of them. *You will marry no one*, he had said.

What will we do?

Silence. Waves slapping indifferently against the hull.

Her words then were deliberate and carefully chosen. In the new religion, she said, hand-fast marriages are permitted when there is no one to perform the ceremony.

But the marriage will not be legal, Michel protested, looking away. His perfect teeth worked at his lower lip. What will he do to me? Now that he knows.

Marguerite persisted. If we place our hands on the New Testament and swear, in God's eyes, we will be married.

Humiliation made her brazen. And once I am carrying your child, none of the other noblemen will want me. Uncle will have no choice. He will have to accept it, then marry us publicly and welcome the addition of a wedded couple and their child to his colony. We must do it soon, Michel. Tonight.

Their marriage was like *un divertissement* performed at court: Marguerite in her rose silk gown, Michel in his soldier's doublet, yellow beeswax candles, Marguerite's New Testament, a bit of bread and wine, all within the cabin, and a fretful Damienne as both lookout and witness, their only guest.

Marguerite pronounced the words: Wilt thee take…honour and cherish…this is my body…this is my blood.

Then Damienne withdrew and they lay together, their loving both sweet and desperate, infused with the thrill of the forbidden.

The next day Marguerite kept her hand to her cheek and carefully avoided her uncle, although she was now more fearful for Michel than for herself. If Roberval hanged him, there would be no marriage. But surely, she told herself, the viceroy would not dare to hang a nobleman.

That evening Jacques Cartier's ships sailed through the narrows and into the harbour, diverting Roberval's attention from his ward and her lover. The colonists were jubilant, but Marguerite could see the hard questions in the set of her uncle's jaw.

When Cartier boarded the *Vallentyne*, Roberval greeted him coldly. Why are you not at Charlesbourg Royal? he asked.

Cartier struggled to be deferential, a muscle twitching at the corner of his mouth. Perhaps we should speak privately, he said, glancing at the expectant faces of those who had gathered around him.

Why are you not at Charlesbourg Royal? Roberval repeated.

Marguerite stepped closer.

Cartier spread his hands, palms empty. Because we are returning to France, he said. There is not enough food for another winter. I have already lost too many men to hunger and sickness.

He leaned closer to Roberval. And to Indians, Cartier said quietly.

Indians. Even the word made Marguerite's belly churn.

You will return with us to Charlesbourg Royal, said Roberval.

Cartier shook his head. *Non*, we will not. It is far too late in the summer to plant. And the Indians will not help us. They will kill us all if they can. We should all return to France.

The low murmuring ceased; ruddy cheeks paled. Trembling fingers pulled at ragged beards, then trailed across mouths that were drawn and pinched.

Marguerite saw fear to match her own.

Roberval's pilot, Jean Alphonse de Saintogne, stepped forward. He opened his mouth, but a venomous look from Roberval stopped the words on his tongue. The assembled noblemen put their hands behind their backs and shifted from one foot to the other. Marguerite heard a sheep's plaintive baa.

I order you to return to Charlesbourg Royal, said Roberval, his voice as sharp and abrasive as ice.

You are mad, Cartier whispered.

As Viceroy of New France, I order you.

Cartier nodded once to acknowledge the pilot, then turned on his heel and disembarked. One of his own men rowed him back to his ship.

By dawn Cartier and his ships were gone, vanished into darkness and grey fog.

Marguerite was now even more heartsick and terrified, worried not only about her and Michel, but about the fate of the entire colony. If the great adventurer Jacques Cartier had abandoned the expedition, what hope was there for them?

Michel tried to reassure her. Roberval is a cruel man, he acknowledged, but King François must have had sound reasons for making your uncle Viceroy of New France. He is a hard leader, but he must know what he is doing.

Did he know what he was doing when he slapped me? she retorted. What does my uncle know of growing grain and raising sheep? Of Indians? And what about us, Michel? What will he do to us?

Marguerite and Michel did their best to stay out of sight and to avoid provoking the viceroy, but in his fury at Cartier, Roberval seemed to have forgotten them. He did not, as they had expected, put them onto separate ships, and he said nothing more to Marguerite about marriage. In fact, he hardly spoke to her at all.

Foolishly Marguerite imagined that her uncle was reconsidering, that his heart was softening.

La demoiselle naïve. La demoiselle bête.

"*Oui,*" I answer, "she was a stupid, stupid girl."

Roberval's discipline became even more severe. He allowed only selected nobles to go ashore, and he regularly threatened the felons with hanging. He swore that King François himself would hang Jacques Cartier when he arrived in France.

How the king would know that Cartier had defied the viceroy, Marguerite wasn't sure, but then she quickly realized that Cartier assumed they would all die: the fate of the colony would vindicate his decision.

Finally, after nearly four weeks in St. John's, Roberval's ships departed for Charlesbourg Royal.

I hear a loud thumping. The Franciscan, his arm raised, blocks the light from the doorway. His cassock snaps in the wind. "Have you forgotten our meeting?" Annoyance rides high atop his words.

"I have forgotten everything...and nothing."

"Do not be coy," he says. His hat bobs, the wide brim caught by the wind. Thevet removes it to swipe a sleeve across his damp brow. He stinks of sweat and impatience. "Let us proceed at once to the chapel." He re-positions his hat, then turns and strides away, assuming my assent.

I watch the billowing cassock recede and consider again the order from King François II. Reluctantly I stand and follow.

Outside, the sky is a smooth undappled grey. A few fat raindrops strike my face. This wind is nothing. I have walked in winds so fierce I could not breathe, winds that drove ice pellets into my face so that my reddened cheeks stung for hours, winds so cold my eyelashes froze, stitched together by my tears.

This wind is nothing. Nothing. The Franciscan is nothing.

Keeping a hand on his hat, André Thevet looks from one side to the other, uneasy to be in Nontron, where, despite Henri's *Chambre Ardente* and Catherine de Medici's harsh measures, there are many

Huguenots. A few men and women stare at the monk as he passes. Everyone in Nontron knows why he is here, and they wonder what I am telling him, if I am answering the questions they are too timid to ask themselves.

A skeletal cur creeps out from an alley. She follows Thevet, snarling and snapping at his heels. He kicks her away, fear pulling hard at his mouth.

I know the bitch from my nighttime wanderings. Like me, she is hungry, but harmless.

Thevet hurries into the sanctuary of the chapel. Out of breath and puffing, he kneels before the crucifix and crosses himself. He gives me a sidelong glance, expecting me to do the same.

Quiet laughter echoes off the stone wall behind the cross: *Hear, O Lord, my prayer…Turn not thy face from me.* I hear ravens calling: *cark-cark-cark.*

The Franciscan does not hear, and he does not see the sacrificed son raise his head and wink. He does not see the pointed pink tongue lapping blood from the nailed feet.

Thevet rises and enters our small chamber. I take my place on the bench opposite the desk. He lights a candle from the banked coals in the hearth, then lights three more. The amber stink of tallow fills the room.

He settles in his chair, smoothes his cassock, and considers his notes. Today he is righteous and does not caress his crotch. "Where were we? Ah, yes." His smile is oily. "We'd arrived at the point in the story where you'd taken a lover and then engaged in wanton and shameless passions…carnal abominations."

"They were married, *Père*."

"Roberval never granted permission. He told me that himself." Thevet draws himself up, proud of his friendship with the Viceroy of New France. "And under French law," he continues, as if lecturing a schoolgirl, "a marriage contracted without your guardian's consent is invalid. So *non*, Marguerite, you were not married. You engaged in an illegitimate union."

He gives a small incredulous laugh. "How could you imagine you were free to choose?" He dips a brown quill into ink. "When did Roberval choose to punish you?"

"It was mid-summer when he put them ashore."

A day of clear blue skies and brisk winds. Just seven days after the ships left St. John's, Roberval ordered the pilot to guide the *Vallentyne* into a deep harbour within a cluster of islands. Men muttered to each other, puzzled, knowing they had not yet arrived at Charlesbourg Royal.

"What happened?"

Shrill voices: *Roberval. Le comportement indécent. Roberval. La putain. Le scandale terrible.*

I put my hands over my ears. I cannot answer. And I cannot forget.

Roberval ordered everyone to gather. Step forward, Marguerite de la Roque de Roberval, he said. It is the appointed time for you to be duly punished for the terrible scandal you have brought upon the honourable name of Roberval.

Coldness in the alabaster face, ice in the blue eyes.

Marguerite looked around desperately for Michel, spotted him standing off to the side, his face as grey as the rope to which he clung.

Did you imagine that we did not see your lascivious behaviour? said Roberval. Your brazen and impudent indecency?

A few of the murderers and thieves sniggered.

Stepping slowly toward her uncle, Marguerite feared she was about to be flogged, laid bare before the prisoners, the leather biting into her back.

Le sang rouge. La pénitence, l'humiliation.

I rock back and forth on the bench.

"Put your hands down and tell me what happened."

I wrap my arms around my waist and continue to rock.

Whore, Roberval pronounced, you shall be put ashore on the Isle of Demons – to be tormented by lost and wicked souls like your own. And because Damienne has acted to protect your indecency, she shall be put ashore with you. I shall not stain my own hands with your blood. I now put your fates in the hands of God.

Hands of God. O Lord, rebuke me not...nor chastise me in thy wrath. Hands of God. Save me for thy mercy's sake. La putain. Whore. Les mains de Dieu.

"Roberval left some biscuit, three arquebuses..."

Marguerite watched in disbelief as a small boat was loaded with supplies and her few possessions: her trunk, her New Testament, her cloak.

The assembled noblemen did not move or say a word. They stood, shoulders slumped forward, soft clean hands crossed in front of their codpieces. Their downcast eyes slid away from hers. Only Jean Alphonse de Saintogne had the courage to approach Roberval. This time the pilot would not be discouraged by the viceroy's malevolent gaze.

Face flushed with alarm, hands outstretched and pointing, the pilot shook his head. The buzzing in her ears was so loud that Marguerite could not hear his words, saw only his mouth moving: *non, non, non*.

When Saintogne's arguments could not dissuade Roberval, Michel stepped forward.

"...a few tools, torn sails..."

"How did it transpire that your lover was put ashore with you?"

"...her trunk, an axe..."

"Marguerite, look at me." The loudness of Thevet's voice startles. "Roberval intended to punish only you. Why was the young man left with you?"

I rub the wound on my wrist, press a thumb down upon it, comforted to feel a familiar pain. "Husband. He was her husband." I gather myself in. "He was an honourable man. When he insisted that he be put ashore with Marguerite and Damienne, Roberval relented."

I stare into the candle's flame and see jade eyes flecked with gold, haunted and grim. Weeks later, when Marguerite would rather have believed in Michel's courage and honour, he confessed to her that he had feared the viceroy would abandon him on a different island or order him to be drowned or hanged.

"His name. What was his name?"

"He brought his own arquebus, his fusil and citre."

"A citre? Your young man was a musician?"

"*Oui.*" But there was only silence and Damienne's whimpering sobs in the boat that took them ashore. No music, just the quiet dipping of oars in dark water, the creaking of wood against wood, the oarsman's grunts, the scrape of the boat against rock when they landed. The oarsman hastily unloaded their meagre provisions, his eyes flinching away from theirs to scan the rocky shore and barren hills, as if he expected to see the Devil himself.

The three said nothing as they watched the boat return to the *Vallentyne*, nothing as they watched the sails of the ship disappear.

Still disbelieving, Marguerite poked among the provisions piled upon the rocks: torn sails, hemp rope, an axe, mallet, and bucket of nails, three arquebuses, powder, and shot, fishing line and hooks, an iron pot, two baskets of hard bread and a small cask of salt beef. Slowly the realization came to her that her uncle had been planning this punishment for days, perhaps weeks. In cold and calculating measures he had drawn up his list and made ready his retribution for her disobedience. How could she have imagined his heart was softening? The screeching gulls mocked her.

Le comportement indécent. Le scandale. Abandoned. Punished.

The twelfth day of July in 1542: the day that Roberval abandoned Marguerite, Michel, and Damienne on the Isle of Demons.

The twelfth day of July in 1542: the day that King François I declared war on the Holy Roman Empire – and lost all interest in Roberval's adventures in New France.

I hear ravens murmuring: *km-mm-mm.*

"His name, Marguerite. What was his name?"

Terrified, Marguerite tried to draw comfort from Michel. Roberval would not truly abandon you, his beloved cousin, he reasoned. A few days to show you his outrage, a week at most. He smiled then. The viceroy has called this place the Isle of Demons only to frighten us, he said, trying to laugh. In just a few days Roberval will send a ship. You will see.

Marguerite did not contradict him, but she did her own calculations: two baskets of hard bread, a cask of salt beef, fishing line and hooks, three muskets, powder, and shot. Roberval did not intend to return for them soon.

"His name, Marguerite. What was his name?"

"*Le jeune homme bête.*"

"Stupid young man," Thevet repeats pointedly. "Very well then. You force me to inform King François of your disobedience." The monk heaves an angry frustrated sigh, reaches for a knife, and begins to sharpen quills. He believes he is giving me time to reflect upon my recalcitrance.

I float above and consider the balding circle at the crown of his head. I see the short list he has made on his paper: *mid-summer, Isle of Demons, Damienne, arquebus, hard bread, citre.* I see myself rocking back and forth, wringing my hands, trying to hold securely between my palms the memories I dare not release to the Franciscan. If I do not keep my hands clutched tightly together, they might reach for his throat, and then, I could not stop them.

A thumb unclenches. A memory slips out through the tiny gap.

While Marguerite and Damienne huddled together, Michel searched the shore and then assured them he'd seen no signs of wolves, monsters, or Indians. No signs of demons.

But I have found a level grassy place at the bottom of an inlet, he said. There is a stream with sweet water. I can use the sails to build shelters there.

When Marguerite bent to lift a basket of biscuit, Michel leapt forward and stayed her hands. *Non, non*, he said, this is not work for a lady. I will move everything.

So while Marguerite and Damienne followed behind, holding their skirts high above the clear green water threatening to lap at their toes, Michel carried the basket of hard bread the short distance to the inlet. Damienne's trembling fingers clung to Marguerite's arm as they watched him make trip after trip, until everything had been moved. Michel grabbed the axe then and strode off. He returned with stout poles he'd cut from trees in a narrow valley farther inland. Using the poles and the hemp rope, he built two rough shelters from the torn sails. By the time he had finished, the sky behind them was a rosy pink.

There is much sweet water, he said, everywhere, and I've seen the trails of rabbits. And foxes. No sign of *les sauvages*. We will be fine.

Michel made a fire from driftwood and dry boughs, and they supped that evening on hard bread and salt beef.

Beneath a cobalt sky and an iron sickle of moon, they retired to canvas shelters and make-shift beds. Giving his sabre to Damienne, Michel took with him his arquebus and dagger.

He whispered assurances to Marguerite and tried to soothe her, but she was too frightened to find comfort in his caresses, too fretful to respond to his kisses.

Eventually the rhythmic slap of wave on rock lulled them to sleep, an uneasy slumber soon disturbed by eerie warbling cries riding atop the wind's soft breath. Damienne scrambled from her shelter into theirs. Michel readied one of the muskets, and Marguerite, fearing demons, grabbed her New Testament and prayed. Clutching the sabre, Damienne sat and moaned, her wails nearly as loud as the warbling cries.

In the morning, Damienne could not be persuaded to venture outside. Despite both her and Michel's protests, Marguerite insisted upon going with Michel to explore the island, to discover its inhabitants, hostile or otherwise. After a hasty breakfast of hard bread and water, they set out, armed with an arquebus, fusil, and dagger.

Less than twenty-five fathoms from the shelters, they found a quiet pool where a pair of sleek black and white birds glided, low and silent upon the water. When one opened its pointed black bill and released a demonic warble, they realized that the birds were the source of the night's haunting calls. They laughed nervously to each other and spoke of Damienne's relief when they told her.

Laboriously loading the musket, Michel shot at one of the birds, but both dived, and neither he nor Marguerite could see where they surfaced again.

Would you teach me? Marguerite asked.

Michel shook his head. *Non*, it would not be proper.

But it would be good if both of us to knew how to shoot, she protested, in case of wild animals or Indians or...

Michel looked off in the distance, sighed, and then handed her the musket. Marguerite could hardly lift the heavy weapon. Thirteen steps to load and shoot, pouring and tamping powder, fire-steel at hand to light the fuse. And the same for the smaller gun, the fusil. They did not yet worry about conserving powder and shot.

I hear the explosion of the long musket and feel the tremendous recoil against my shoulder, the jolt pulling me back into my body, back into the Franciscan's agitated presence. Sharpening his quills,

Thevet has remained unusually silent.

After the shooting lesson, Michel and Marguerite returned to tell a sceptical Damienne about the birds. Still, she would not budge from the shelter.

Michel and Marguerite continued their explorations. Near shore they found small patches of scraggly spruce and fir, all bent away from the sea as if repulsed, or afraid. Taller trees grew in the valleys, trunks close and branches interlaced as if embracing each other. Michel and Marguerite came upon wet grassy meadows dotted with daisies and buttercups, and they discovered mossy bogs with scattered low shrubs bearing bright pink blossoms. The soft green moss exuded a fragrance Marguerite found peculiar but pleasant, an aroma both clean and musky.

Startling them, a partridge burst from the dense shrubs growing at the edge of a bog, but was gone too quickly for Michel even to raise the fusil.

They climbed the high granite domes in the centre of the island and from there surveyed their domain. From that vantage point, the island looked like one solid rock, an ancient turtle's arched back laced with grey and red ridges. Dark pools and bogs lay in the depressions; short trees stood thick in the valleys. They could see at least a dozen rocky islands nearby, as well as scores of smaller ones, some no more than an outcropping of stone in a sparkling sea.

Michel rotated in a complete circle, then pulled at his dark beard. I believe we are standing on the largest island, he said, perhaps two miles long and about the same wide, though it is hard to judge.

He held both arms straight out, then brought an open hand to his brow. All to the south and east, he said, reckoning by the sun.

They turned. To the northwest, at least two or three miles distant, they could see a larger landmass. Another island? New France? They couldn't tell.

No matter what direction they turned, however, they could see no white sails.

In all of their explorations, and much to everyone's relief, Marguerite and Michel saw no signs of demons or Indians, and Michel tried not to worry that he'd also seen little in the way of animal tracks or spoor, only a few trails made by rabbits and foxes.

Later that day, Michel used the fishing line and hooks, baiting the hook with a tiny scrap of salt beef. His catch was meagre, two flatfish, which they roasted over the fire, along with a few whelks Marguerite had collected in the pools left by the retreating tide.

That evening Michel set snares in the runs he'd seen, and by dawn two rabbits dangled in leather nooses. Marguerite, after she'd gathered her hair within her pearl snood and fashioned a bonnet against the sun, allowed herself a brief and delicate sorrow for their large amber eyes.

Michel dressed the rabbits, running his dagger the length of their tawny bellies and tossing the bowels to the screeching gulls. They roasted the slender bodies and picked apart the flesh with their fingers. Certain they'd be on the island only a few more days at most, Michel did not bother to save the skins or the bones.

La folie. La stupidité. How long, O Lord? How long?

The scrape of the Franciscan's knife against the quill's nib punctuates the words and chuckling laughter. The monk does not look up from his work. He is giving me more time to contemplate her sins – and mine.

Marguerite prayed. Every morning and evening she prayed for their rescue. She sang the psalms she'd learned as a child.

Her sweet voice sounds in my head: *I will love thee, O Lord, my strength. The Lord is my firmament, my refuge, and my deliverer. My God is my helper, and in him will I put my trust.*

Other voices join in a mocking chorus: *My strength. My deliverer. Kek-kek-kek. Km-mm-mm.*

"My strength," I mutter. Thevet looks up from his quills, his broad pig's forehead furrowed. I study my clasped hands.

How long, O Lord? How long? Saved by our grace, not God's.

Over the next few days Damienne, who refused to venture more than a hundred paces from the shelters, began grumbling incessantly. She had an endless stream of laments. The salt meat is nearly gone, she fretted, and we have only tasteless rabbit, stringy partridge, fish, and hard bread. No wine, no cheese, no nuts of any kind. And the few berries I've found are hard and sour. And probably poisonous, she added.

She complained about sleeping on the hard ground and about the bugs that descended whenever the wind stilled. Their droning whine and stinging bites sometimes drove them all into the stifling heat of the canvas shelters, faces and hands covered with angry red welts.

Damienne gasped and trembled at every loud noise, and although they'd heard in the night only the quavering calls of the black and white birds, the sighing wind, and the rhythmic slap of waves, Damienne spoke often of her terror of wild animals and monsters, demons and *les sauvages*.

But Michel and I have walked all over the island and seen no sign of demons or Indians, Marguerite insisted, annoyed that Damienne's chatter brought to mind fears she had worked to banish. Marguerite had willed herself to trust what Michel had said: her uncle had called this place the Isle of Demons only to frighten them, and he would not allow his beloved cousin to die.

For her and for Michel, now convinced of Roberval's imminent return, their abandonment became the great adventure. They began to think of themselves as Adam and Eve in the garden. The skies remained a crystalline blue; golden grasses and white daisies bowed and danced in a gentle wind. Michel played his citre under the open sky, the soft notes of love songs blending with the piping of grey and white birds and the soughing trees.

And they loved. Marguerite and Michel loved within the canvas shelter and on the soft dry mosses; they loved in the broad meadows where the wind dried their sweat-slicked bodies. There was no one but Damienne to see or to hear, and they loved openly and wildly, sometimes pretending they were deer.

They were ravenous for each other. They could not love enough, and no part of Marguerite remained untouched by Michel's tongue, and she tasted him, salt and berries. She breathed in the grassy fragrance of his skin together with the scents of sweet mosses and pungent fir.

In the rain pocking on the window, I hear drumming on canvas. I feel Michel's smooth belly against her back, his fingers teasing nipples thirsty for the touch of his tongue, his hardness against her. Strong hands grasp her hips and pull her to him. Her back arches as he enters from behind. Later, standing, her soft skin scrapes against hard rock, not caring, because her legs are wrapped around his waist, his mouth is on her neck as he plunges into the greedy hollow within.

I close my eyes and recall sitting astride, breasts bared to the sun's lecherous eye, breath coming in gasps, crying out to the taffeta clouds above. My eyes flutter open.

The Franciscan is staring at me, his face pinched, his hands folded over his cock. He picks up a quill and dips it into black ink. "And that is when your young man built the canvas shelter?"

"He built two. But the wind was the serpent."

"The serpent?"

"The serpent in the garden."

Thevet arches a thick eyebrow. "And you, no

doubt, were the temptress." He comes around the desk to stand before me, too close. I can smell the stale wool of his cassock, his sour skin.

He lays a hand upon my shoulder. "How long did you and your lover live in the canvas shelters?" His hot fingers caress my neck.

I sweep his hand from my shoulder.

He steps back. His bulbous eyes travel slowly over my breasts. He nods in affirmation. "*Oui*, the temptress," he says. "Eve in the garden."

Thevet returns to his seat behind the desk and lays his folded hands upon the papers. "How long, Marguerite, did you and your lover live in the shelters?"

I hear winds howling, ravaging, battering. "A fortnight," I say, "until the winds became too strong."

The canvas could not withstand such adversarial winds, winds so fierce Marguerite could hardly walk against them. It was then that she knew why the small twisted spruce bent away from the sea.

"What did you do then?"

"Her husband had discovered a cave. They retreated to that."

"Not husband, Marguerite. You had joined yourselves in a libidinous and illegitimate union."

The cat dangles in the noose, legs kicking. I reach to twist her neck, just like a rabbit's. Then I see her green eyes: terror, rage. Eyes like his. But unlike Michel, she fights to live. She claws and scratches. I cannot kill her.

I grab the dagger and slide the tip beneath the leather thong. The noose snaps open, and she is gone. I pull down the snare and throw the leather scraps to the street below. I put out a piece of cheese I was saving for my supper. I will go hungry.

The scratches on my hands burn.

The girls are practising making letters. Squeak of chalk on slate, like the scrape of stone upon stone, pale lines on a smoke-darkened wall, keeping count.

How long, O Lord? How long? For my days are vanished like smoke.

I dreamed last night of the cave, of a white bear. I could hear the *huff-huff-huff* and smell the stink of rotting seal. I crouched under a ledge. Though the entrance was too small for the bear, I was terrified. A shaggy paw snaked in. I pulled a burning brand from the fire and touched the yellow flame to white fur. The enraged howl woke me. The odour of singed fur lingered.

"What happened to your hands?" Isabelle asks.

I fold them together to hide the scratches. "Rabbits," I say. "For supper."

She cocks her head momentarily and then with a shrug of her small shoulders dismisses her curiosity. Something is puzzling Isabelle far more than the scratches on my hands.

"Do you believe God cares what we eat?" she asks. "Papa says that on certain days we can only eat fish. He says that's what God wants." Her nose wrinkles. "I don't like fish."

I think of fish: raw, burnt, half-rotten, slimy and stinking. Marguerite ate it all, every scrap. She sucked the bones and ate the heads, the skin, the tails, the fins, sometimes gagging and trying not to chew – and never considered whether she liked it or not.

I want to tell Isabelle that God doesn't give a damn if we eat at all – or if we starve. Instead I say, "You must obey your papa. It is not for us to understand what God demands of us."

"Papa says that sometimes he is testing us."

I clench my teeth to hold back what Monsieur Lafrenière would surely consider blasphemy: What kind of father tests his most loving and obedient children – and then condemns those who fail?

Marguerite believed that God tests the righteous, and after several weeks on the island she concluded that, like Job, she was being tested. I hear again her prayers: *Be thou unto me a God, a protector, and a house of refuge…They were hungry and thirsty…And they cried to the Lord in their tribulation, and he delivered them out of their distresses.*

And when she grew more afraid and more desperate: *Have mercy on me, O Lord, for I am weak…Turn to me, O Lord, and deliver my soul. O save me for thy mercy's sake.*

But he did not deliver them out of their distresses.

He did not save them. And if God was testing Marguerite, if God found her faith wanting, then God is a fool.

Isabelle leans closer. Her perfect lips whisper, "But if God loves us, like Papa says, why is he so mean? Why does he make us eat fish?" She takes a shuddering breath. "Why did he let Mama die?"

Isabelle returns to her bench and picks up her slate.

After they moved to the cave, Marguerite no longer felt like Eve in the garden. She began thinking more about Job and a faith tested. She picked up a sharp stone and began cutting lines into red granite walls not yet blackened by soot.

We must not forget the sabbath, she said, or the saints' days.

She read her New Testament daily. And she prayed. Marguerite implored God to send a ship, any ship. And every day, without fail, Michel built a fire on the beach, adding green boughs so that grey smoke billowed heavenward.

No ship came. Only the wind.

Wind and rain flail against the window. The Franciscan pours wine, dark and red, liquid rubies in the candlelight. I stare into a small flame and think of Isabelle's rosy lips, her skin like creamy silk. I hear an infant's whimper, then only the moan and clatter of wind and rain.

The cheese was gone this morning. I put out a small bone, a scrap of rabbit still attached.

Thevet rattles a paper. "Where was the cave?"

"Near the centre of the island."

"How big was it?"

"About two body lengths' long. Not quite as wide." Hardly big enough for the three of them to lie down at the same time. A second, sloping chamber toward the back where Marguerite could keep her trunk.

"There was one small area high enough for a person to stand, but they built the fire there, so the smoke could escape."

The Franciscan scribbles down my words. I do not bother explaining that Michel took the poles from the shelters, and with the precious few nails they had, he blocked one entrance and made the other more narrow to keep out the wind and cold.

"What did you eat?"

"Rabbits, partridge, fish, mussels, berries, gulls." Michel fashioned a small net from twine. He used offal for bait then hid behind rocks and waited: ten throws for every gull caught. The gulls became wary, screaming their fear and rage. Then fifty throws for every gull caught.

"Seal?"

I nod. Michel tried to shoot the seals that basked on the rocks, but even when his aim was true, their grey forms slipped from the smooth surface and sank before he could retrieve them. Later, much later, Marguerite and Damienne ate whatever stinking carcass washed up on shore.

The monk sits back and makes a tent with his fingers, his lecturing pose. "*Oui*," he says, "I know from my own travels to Terra Neuve–"

"Nova," I say. "Terra Nova...Terre Neuve."

Thevet sucks his teeth, annoyed at being interrupted, and corrected. "As I was saying," he continues, "this country is inhabited by barbarians clothed in wild animal skins. Intractable, ungracious, and unapproachable, unless by force...as those who go there to fish for cod will attest. They live almost exclusively on fish, especially seals, whose flesh is very good and delicate to them. Or so I've been told by Cartier."

I smell tallow and think of a dead seal wedged between rocks, rancid, rotten, the meat already slimy. Marguerite had to fight off ravens and gulls.

The monk blathers on, not hearing how the rhythm of his words ill-fits the rain's drumming. "They make a certain oil from the fat of this fish, which, after being melted, has a reddish colour." He lifts his chalice and sips dramatically. "They drink it with their meals as we here would drink wine or water. And they make coats and clothing from its skin."

Lecture finished for now, he considers me. "But you were there for more than two years, alone for nearly a year." His forehead creases. "How did you survive?"

Thin white lines on smoke-blackened walls: eight hundred and thirty-two. Scrape of stone upon stone. I hear them then: *How long, O Lord? How long? For my days are vanished like smoke, and my bones are grown dry like fuel for the fire.*

"She also ate roots, seaweed. Bark."

"How could you possibly survive on that?"

I taste salty bitter herbs. And blood. Sharp edges of bark cut the tongue. "She didn't."

The voices intertwine gracefully within the wind and rain: *Grievous sin. La culpabilité. Impardonnable. Kek-kek-kek. Saved by our grace, not God's.*

His eyes are slits, like the eyes of a serpent feigning sleep. "What do you mean?" he says.

"Marguerite died. I lived."

"I don't understand."

"Of course not."

He clutches the gold cross that lies nestled against his breast. When he finally speaks, his voice is tight, as if my hands are squeezing his throat. "Roberval knew, and you have said yourself that the island is well populated with demons. Were you seduced by the Devil? Did he grant you life in exchange for your soul?"

Thevet holds out the cross like a shield. His voice rises in accusation. "Is that how you survived? By witchcraft? Is that how you sought revenge against your uncle?"

I touch the blade of the dagger and imagine slicing his face and watching blood drip from his trembling chin onto his papers.

"Christ expelled seven demons from Mary Magdalene," he says quickly. "How many do you harbour, Marguerite? How many?"

If my lips were not stone, I would smile. "If I had those powers, *Père*, would I be sitting here with you?"

He shrinks back into his chair. "The Devil works in mysterious ways."

"I thought that was God."

I sit among the trees' welcoming embrace. Their trunks and branches are like silver threads sewn into the black satin of night. Water drips from new leaves. I clutch shards of broken pottery, bits of clay painted with pale blue forget-me-nots. I found the shards in a rubbish heap. I had to chase away the pig rooting for turnip scrapings and rotten cabbage.

Marguerite would have used the shards as chess pieces. Bored and restless, she meticulously lined up small stones to form a chessboard on the broad flat rock beside the cave. She searched for coloured and distinctive stones and then made them into kings, queens, knights, bishops, rooks, and pawns. Michel teased and called her foolish, but he smiled, and in the long twilight between their meagre evening meal and nightfall, he allowed her to teach him how to play.

A large clay bowl. Who would be so careless as to break it? Marguerite would have traded her pearl ring for such a bowl. She would have traded her ring for the shards.

Rose silk. An ebony feather, a pearl ring. The scent of moss.

I lift my nose and sniff. I am eighty miles from the sea, but I can still smell salt, can still hear waves pummelling rock, a relentless wearing away. And then I hear it, a *citre*, the simple elegant notes of a *pavane* straining to rise above the sea's bleak howl. While Michel played, Marguerite danced around the fire, her movements slow and graceful, the wind billowing her skirts, her chestnut curls falling thick and loose. She'd stopped wearing the snood by now and simply tied her hair back with a satin ribbon. When she danced, she let her hair fall loose, and Michel looked upon her with admiration and desire.

As more and more weeks passed and no ship came, Michel stopped playing the citre. No longer smiling indulgently, he began to chastise Marguerite when she asked him to play. He kicked at her chessboard, grinding the pieces under his boots. And he no longer cared how hard she worked – or if the work was proper for a lady. He began to scoff when she prayed.

I stretch out my legs and rub my arms for warmth. There was hardly room in the cramped cave for all of them to lie down. With Damienne so near, Michel and Marguerite were circumspect, confining their love-making to the woods and open meadows. Even then, Michel was far less free in his attentions, his once-buoyant spirits weighed down, melancholy and angry humours growing within. Marguerite tried to flirt and tease, stroking his chest and untying the lacings of his shirt. She ran her fingers through his beard, an unkempt tangled mass, no longer a neatly trimmed triangle. Michel swept her hands away and stared at the roiling sea.

Too late in the year, he said. Roberval has gone on to Charlesbourg Royal. He cannot send a ship until spring. How can we survive until spring?

Now it was Marguerite's turn to offer assurances. The viceroy was angry and wanted to punish me, she acknowledged. But he is my protector. I am his ward, his beloved cousin. He will come. You will see.

And, she added brightly, at least there are no demons, no Indians. She lifted her hands to cup Michel's cheeks, but then dropped them to her sides, alarmed by the dark anger she saw.

Marguerite never lost faith in Roberval's intention to rescue her, but when more weeks passed and he did not send a ship, she began to fear for his life, anxious that the ships had foundered and that her uncle had drowned.

Never could she have imagined his hardness of heart. Never could she have imagined that he wanted her to die.

Le bâtard meurtrier.

"*Oui,*" I agree, "murderous bastard."

I think of the Queen of Navarre. You can do nothing, she said. Roberval is viceroy, the law in New France. You must leave it to God to punish him.

Leave it to God. Km-mm-mm.

Would that I had the powers of a witch. I would have killed him at the first opportunity.

Debts must be paid.

I nod. *Oui,* debts must be paid.

My dark soul would have traveled at night when my body was asleep. To Paris, to the Church of the Innocents. I would have used Michel's dagger to slit his throat. I run a finger along the sharp edge of the pottery shard and imagine blue forget-me-nots floating in a pool of scarlet.

If I did not do it, why can I see it all so clearly: Roberval, his ice-blue eyes wide with terror, a gaping grin from ear to ear, blood covering my hands, dripping through my fingers? Why do the scents of blood and salt lace my dreams?

Dawn: grey ashy wool. I wake hunched, my back against a tree, my cloak wrapped around my shoulders and knees. My hand has released the shards to the ground. Legs stiff, I rise awkwardly. The cloak's hem carries barbed seeds, and I begin to pick them off. Then stop. I will carry them back to Nontron and scatter them in gardens. Can wild unruly things live in such tamed places, within the security of rock walls? I drop the hem of my cloak, pick up the shards, and pull the rough wool closer in.

Wool. Crouched in the cave, Marguerite opened her trunk and considered the creamy satin and rose silk. She wanted to slide the rich fabrics between her fingertips and feel the soft silk and smooth satin on her cheeks, but she dared not touch them now with her rough hands and ragged nails. She looked at the costly gowns, then she wished for wool, of any colour, and a spinning wheel and loom, so she could make warm cloaks and sturdy breeches. Her thin chemise and cotton gowns had become tattered, her white linen cuffs filthy and fraying. She'd stopped wearing her stiffened stomacher only days after they were abandoned. Here on the island it seemed a foolish contrivance, especially when Damienne or Michel had to lace it tight every morning and then loosen it at night.

She carefully elbowed aside the silk and satin, then rummaged in the trunk, searching for something useful. Marguerite was glad that she had no looking glass to reflect her darkened face and chapped lips – glad that she could not see in her own eyes the despair she saw in Michel's and Damienne's.

The cave was silent, save for the sounds of her own rustling. Even in the long nights when they huddled in the cave together, there were only the sounds of the fire's crackle and hiss, the dull clunk of wood stacked upon wood, the crack and pop of Damienne's joints. Michel no longer played his citre. It crouched beneath a stone ledge like a shunned child.

From the day of their abandonment, they had avoided speaking of hopes and plans for their lives in New France, but they had asked each other for songs and ballads and amusing stories about their friends and their childhoods. Damienne had rattled on endlessly about the merits of her long-dead husband, and in an intimate moment, told Marguerite about a stillborn son. They occasionally discussed religion and politics and wondered aloud about life at court.

But now, weeks later, they had ceased to speak altogether, as if confinement had made them too familiar. They grunted and pointed, mumbled only to themselves.

Marguerite continued, however, to talk to God. I will love thee, O Lord, she prayed, my strength… Have mercy on me, O Lord, for I am weak…O save me for thy mercy's sake.

All of them stank of sweat and grime and blood. What use to dip white linen collars and cuffs in water and beat them against rocks when they had no soap? What use to wash anything, even their own hands and faces?

They'd also begun to carry the stink of fear. The cave hoarded their stench as if it were a thing to be savoured.

During long hungry nights, Marguerite could think only of food: bread, cheese, roasted pig, apples, honeyed hazelnuts, wine. Scarcely able to believe it now, she recalled evenings when she'd been so full she'd turned away from the table and proffered chunks of roasted pig, dripping with fat, to the king's hounds.

Marguerite reached for an ivory box in the corner of the trunk, slid open the cover. Needles. Could she somehow fashion usable clothing from rabbit skins? They'd begun to save them, though she was afraid to consider what that might mean. Were they now reconciled? She shook her head to dismiss the thought. She would not think ahead, would not imagine a winter on the island. It was only the beginning of September. Her uncle would come soon.

In the corner of the trunk, her fingers found a stack of clean muslin rags. How long since she'd needed them? She sat back on her heels and counted the white lines on the dark wall: fifty-two days they had been on the island, and it had been at least several weeks before that.

Marguerite laid her hands on her flat belly. *Non*, it could not be.

I hear an infant's wails. I run toward the sound. But now the cries are behind me. I spin around and run the other way. The wails become whimpers, coming from high in the trees. Then there is only silence and the sound of my own breathing as I suck air deep into my chest. I slump to the cold ground and wait for my breathing to quiet.

If the baby were mine, I would weep. But she was Marguerite's.

I chew on bread and cheese, the bread so tough and dry it pulls at my teeth. When I came back to the garret, I was oddly pleased to find the bone, with its scrap of meat, gone. I decided, quite suddenly, to be wildly wasteful. The decision made me tremble with the eagerness of a young girl. I put a small piece of cheese just outside the window. Around it I scattered a fine dust of ashes, the ash slipping through my fingertips like grey silk. I want to know that it is the yellow-striped cat, and not rats, who is benefiting from my small gifts of food. Has she ceased to fear me?

Fear. In all its guises: worry, terror, despair. Those humours filling the bowels so there is room for nothing else. So quickly did Michel succumb to melancholy and anger, and the soot-black humour of fear.

The evening when Marguerite finally told Michel they had all shared one roasted gull, the meat tough and stringy and tasting of fish. They had also eaten a few mussels and whelks Marguerite had gathered, her skirts bunched up around her waist, the icy water stinging her feet and calves and making her hands ache. Damienne had retired to the cave to give the young couple some privacy by the fire near the harbour, but there were no tender caresses, no loving words.

Marguerite steadied her voice, trying to disguise her own fear. I have counted as best I can, she said. Early April.

Michel bowed his head. None of us will live to see April, he muttered to the bones and shells at his feet.

Non, she said. You will see. A ship will come. I will give birth to our child at Charlesbourg Royal in the company of other colonists, in the company of women who know of such things.

Michel tugged his fingers through his matted beard and barked a harsh laugh. When he looked up at Marguerite, his smirk was cruel. Perhaps, he said, you will have the good fortune to lose the child. Early.

With a sharp intake of breath, Marguerite spun away from him, but too late. She had already seen. Despair had snuffed out his love for her, leaving behind only a faint trail of grey smoke and dark ash.

She turned toward the broad expanse of unforgiving sea and searched amongst the cold waves for a psalm to comfort her. She recited the words almost silently so that Michel would not hear her and mock.

Hear, O Lord, my prayer, she murmured, and let my cry come to thee. Turn not away thy face from me. In the day when I am in trouble, incline thy ear to me…For my days are vanished like smoke, and my bones are grown dry like fuel for the fire.

Turn not away from me. Vanished like smoke. Fuel for the fire. Km-mm-mm.

Shivering, I decide to kindle a fire. It is the sabbath, and I do not have to go downstairs to teach the girls. I do not have to meet with the Franciscan. At dusk, I will walk the woods and fields outside Nontron, but I will stay away from the river. I do not want to hear the sound of water. Ever. I will listen, instead, for the beat of black wings, the raucous croaks and softer *km-mm-mms* that tell me they are there, keeping watch.

Isabelle blows small bursts of air through pursed lips. She scrinches her eyes as she tries to pass yarn through the eye of a blunt needle. Frustrated, she lays the needle down beside the stocking she is darning.

The stocking is lumpy with tangles and knots, and her fingertips are red.

She slides off her bench and walks toward me, takes a pinch of my skirt and tugs. "Madame de Roberval," she says, "why do we never sing? I would like to sing."

I think of Marguerite's gentle voice rising and falling in prayers and psalms, of Michel singing romantic ballads, *les chansons d'amour*.

"And dance," she says excitedly, grabbing my hand. "Papa says you were often at court. You must know how to dance."

"Your father is mistaken. I was never at court." I try not to imagine the other lies he is telling this child.

"But Papa–"

"*Non*," I say, pulling my hand from hers. "Go back to your darning."

"But could we sing?" she persists, her lisp more pronounced. *Could we thing?*

"If you wish to *thing*, you must do so at home. Your papa can teach you. He seems to know every-thing."

Isabelle does not hear the acid in my voice. She looks toward the ceiling and sighs. "He never sings. He's always reading."

Her beautiful lips pout, and I think of Michel's lips, his gay voice, and the music of the citre. When I was taken from the island, the ship's captain took the instrument in exchange for my passage, but even then was reluctant to take me aboard. He could not be convinced I was human. It was only his greed for the citre, with its precious metals and inlaid ivory, that saved me – or condemned me.

Isabelle has returned to her bench. She pushes dark curls away from her face, steals a sidelong glance at me, and then reaches for a chunk of chalk and a roof-slate instead of her yarn and stocking. I leave her alone. I have scolded enough.

Turning away, I allow myself a small smile. This morning the cheese was gone. When I opened the window upstairs, a gust of wind blew ashes into my face, and I tasted grit on my tongue, but not before I saw tracks on the ledge: four rounded toes and a pad, a cat's paws, not a rat's.

What does Monsieur Lafrenière think he knows? What does he want to know? I walk to the narrow window and crack it open so I can breathe.

How long, O Lord? How long? Days vanished like smoke. Grievous sin. La culpabilité.

Memories explode within my skull. My head aches from the reverberations. Hands to my forehead, I stare out on the muddy road. And now I am floating, outside, above the mud, and looking back at the scrivener's shop. I see through the walls, to the girls inside the classroom, heads bent over their darning. All except Isabelle. She works at the slate, the chalk tapping, grating, scraping.

Lines on the granite wall. Scrape of stone upon stone.

Before she knew how to make sinew, Marguerite used twine to sew rabbit skins together. When Michel saw her using his dagger to poke holes in the stiff skins, he carved a bone awl. Without a word, he tossed it into her lap. She had learned when she was a child how to preserve the skins of sheep and rabbits, but the furs she had now – some entirely white, others still tawny but mottled with white – had not been properly tanned. She did not have the tools to work them, to stretch and soften them, and the skins were stiff and her sewing clumsy, but they made a warm cloak. Marguerite also fashioned hoods and crude mitts, and tried not to worry that the rabbits were becoming harder and harder to catch.

Now and again Michel snared a fox or weasel or mink, its fur thick and lustrous, but he refused to wear anything made from the animals' skins.

We are not *les sauvages*, he said, his face bitter. Not yet.

The ducks and gulls were becoming as scarce as the rabbits. Michel baited hooks with bits of their entrails to catch fish from the sea and from the lower pools and streams. He carved a spear that he and Marguerite used to stab flatfish in the shallows and a few salmon in the cold brooks. Damienne, who refused to put a foot in the water, any water, because of her terrible fear of drowning and of monsters, gathered whatever berries and roots she could find without venturing too far from the cave. All three of them were growing thin, even the corpulent Damienne. Their ragged clothes hung loose from their shoulders.

Marguerite's belly had barely begun to round when she finally told the old woman. Damienne's hands fluttered about her gaunt face. She pretended gladness – and a knowledge of birthing she did not have. She struggled to make herself smile, then she fussed and fretted over Marguerite as if this were a joyous event. She chirped and chattered, suggesting that they begin making blankets and bunting from rabbit skins.

Marguerite willed her to be silent. She could not think about the baby. She could think only of how she had lost Michel's love. Her body craved food, but even more the comfort of his touch. She could only dimly recall his dazzling smile, and her ears hungered for the sound of his voice, light and gay and confident once again. At night, when they lay side by side on flat pink stone, feet toward the fire, they could have fed their love. Instead she starved for the feel of his mouth on hers, for the embrace of his arms and the warmth of his body pressed against her.

Michel left her empty and ravenous.

She felt betrayed by her body, and then ashamed. Once, not so long ago, though it now seemed like years, she had wanted this baby. She had thought that her uncle would marry them if she were carrying Michel's child. How foolish she had been.

Marguerite prayed for God's mercy. She prayed for their rescue, and she prayed that Michel's love would return when the ship finally came.

She prayed that he would not scorn her forever.

Continuously, without pause, her lips murmured prayers: Have mercy on me, O Lord...My God is my helper, and in him will I put my trust...They wandered in a wilderness in a place without water. They found not the way of a city for their habitation. They were hungry and thirsty. Their soul fainted in them. And they cried to the Lord in their tribulation, and he delivered them out of their distresses...

How long, O Lord? How long? Whispers. Growls. Taunts. *Out of the depths I have cried to thee. Km-mm-mm. Saved by our grace, not God's.*

I am back in the classroom. I hear giggling behind me, the girls this time, not the voices, but when I turn from the window, they concentrate on their needles and stockings, their faces solemn. The tip of Isabelle's pink tongue covers her upper lip, and she works quietly with the chalk. She does not raise her head, afraid that I will make her pick up her wool and needle.

I turn back to the window. The air is balmy, but I see snow falling and feel sleet and icy pellets strike my face, freezing my eyes.

The days grew short and bitter cold, the winds more fierce, driving ice onto the shore. The ice became so thick they could have walked to nearby islands, but they had neither reason nor will nor energy to do so. Marguerite and Damienne hauled water and driftwood to the cave. They cut spindly dry trees and gathered all the frozen berries they could find, no longer caring that the berries might be poisonous.

Michel left the cave only to check and re-set the snares. He said little, and even then Marguerite and Damienne did not welcome his words, for he could only curse Roberval and mutter about cold, hunger, death, and murder. The weight of his bitterness was worse than the thick smoke-laden air.

Marguerite tried to answer his gruffness with tenderness, but he brushed aside her hands, and her words. They still lay side by side at night, but he denied her even the warmth of his body lying close to hers.

Damienne, her face now deeply lined, her grey hair thin, and her skin dark and scaly, no longer troubled herself to give the lovers privacy. There was no need.

One day, outside the cave, she pulled Marguerite aside. You cannot keep thinking of *him*, she said, not even willing to speak Michel's name. You must think of the baby, and you must not be so sad. Your sadness will hurt the baby.

The baby. Michel would not speak of the baby. Michel did not want the baby. Marguerite tried to convince herself that she did, that the baby was a gift from God, a blessing. She continued to read her New Testament and to pray: Have mercy on me, O Lord, for I am weak…From my mother's womb thou art my God. Depart not from me. For tribulation is very near, and there is none to help me.

Marguerite prayed and she fretted, for she had begun to see the sense of what Michel had said: it would be fortunate to lose the baby, as early as possible. It would be a sin to pray, or even to wish, for such a fate, an even greater sin to act to bring it about. Yet Marguerite, as if dwelling in a body not entirely her own and driven by a will outside of her soul, watched her hands gather roots, seeds, and dried leaves from every plant she could find. She ground and chopped as best she could, then boiled her concoctions in the black pot. Hands shaking, she would bring the dark brews to her lips. There was no sugar or honey to make the draughts less bitter.

Nor should they be less bitter, she thought. It was only right and good that they should make her retch and bring a griping to her bowels.

Pretending that she had been only searching for and preparing food, she offered the foul-tasting mixtures to Michel and Damienne. Michel answered with a low grumble, Damienne with a disapproving scowl, and Marguerite worried that God would know her real intention, her wickedness.

She would drop to her knees then and pray for forgiveness: O Lord, rebuke me not in thy indignation, nor chastise me in thy wrath. Have mercy on me, O Lord, for I am weak.

Mercy upon me, O Lord. Weak, weak, weak. Km-mm-mm.

Marguerite would not compound her sin by holding God accountable.

But I will.

I clasp my hands together to keep them from reaching out and sweeping the lamp to the floor. I would hear it crash and see it shatter. I would use a shard to slice my wrist. Blood. There should be blood.

Was it not a sin for God to have visited such a fate upon her? In the face of her faith, her love and petitions, was it not a sin for him to remain silent?

Out of the depths I have cried to thee...How long, O Lord? How long? Saved by our grace, not God's. Km-mm-mm.

Isabelle looks up from her slate to my tightly folded hands. Her tongue darts over her half-teeth, the ivory squares just coming in. "Madame de Roberval." Her words are soft and hesitant. "Papa says you lived on an island with wolves and bears...and demons."

"*Non.*"

"Papa is wrong?" Her small chin juts out, a challenge.

"Your father is correct in most things," I say carefully. "In this he has simply mistaken me for someone else."

"But he has books," she says with authority. "He reads about wild places. And demons. He says that you were on the Isle of Demons."

"*Non*, that was not me."

Isabelle beckons me closer, cups her small hands around her mouth, and lisps into my ear. "Papa says it was Monsieur de Roberval who was the demon."

I draw back. How does Lafrenière know these stories?

Isabelle draws a small finger across her throat, an imaginary slice. "Papa says it is good that someone killed him. In Paris." She tilts her head, coy now. "I've never been to Paris. Have you?"

"Your papa has mistaken me for someone else," I repeat, my heart beating so hard I fear she will hear it.

"Papa is smart," she retorts. "He reads books about alchemy and geography. He says the king's cosmographer is a fool."

I am startled, and distressed, that Lafrenière knows anything about André Thevet, that he has been talking to Isabelle about Marguerite, about me. Of what interest can the Franciscan be to him?

Of what interest am I?

Isabelle continues to chatter. "Papa tells me that the men who write books about geography say the king's cosmographer has never been to New France. Or Terre Neuve." She looks from side to side, as if one of the other girls might be listening. She lowers her voice. "They say the monk is a liar who makes up stories about Indians."

"Wipe the slate. Now. You must work on your darning."

Isabelle's face falls, as if she had expected me to welcome her confidences, had expected I would want to hear more. On her slate she has drawn a wolf with huge jagged teeth and a woman stabbing it with a spear. Isabelle pouts even more as she wipes a rag over her drawing. She wipes away the pointed teeth last.

Wolves came to the island after the sea had frozen, after the deer had come across the ice. One morning late in December, Michel found a long trail of huge rounded hoofprints in the snow, several animals by his reckoning. Damienne worried that the prints were the tracks of monsters and retreated to the cave.

Although the muskets had ceased to fire reliably,

Michel was able to stalk and kill one of the deer. Returning to the cave with the animal draped across his shoulders, he grinned for the first time in months. Without a word, he laid it before them. Marguerite wept, her tears falling on the buff-coloured neck. She wept again when her teeth bit into the dark-red liver, still running with the animal's warm blood.

Michel dressed the deer, throwing only what was putrid in the bowels to the gulls and ravens. They roasted the meat over the fire and devoured the thick fat on the haunches. Grease dripped from their chins, and their bellies felt full at last.

That night Michel and Marguerite loved. On the pink rock, warmed by the fire, they loved, and Marguerite slept within Michel's embrace.

They saved every part of the deer: hide, antlers, bones, even the contents of its stomach. What meat they could not eat right away, Marguerite and Damienne sliced into thin strips and dried near the fire in the cave.

The deer gave them hope.

Then came the eerie howls in the night, four-toed tracks in the snow as big as Michel's hand, competitors for deer and for the few rabbits and partridge – predators who looked upon them as prey. Michel fortified the entrances to the cave with more stout poles, then he and Marguerite took turns standing guard, watching for copper eyes in the night and the flash of long white teeth.

I hear an explosion reverberate off stone walls. I cringe and my ears ring.

"When did your lover die?" The Franciscan is using a knife to smooth a ragged thumbnail.

"Her husband died on the third day of March in 1543."

The knife stops. "You know exactly?"

"Two hundred and thirty-four days after Roberval left them." Scrape of stone upon stone. Lines counted. Marguerite's belly round and heavy, her legs and arms like sticks, fingernails torn and bleeding as she dug at frozen soil and stones to place his body into a crevice beneath a rock slab one hundred and twenty-two strides back from the cave. It was the rock upon which they climbed to follow the path to the summit or to walk down to the harbour. Nearly every time she left the cave she would place her foot upon his crypt.

They had no linen to spare for a shroud, so Marguerite covered his nakedness in death with the rabbit furs he would not wear in life.

Using large rocks that she had to carry to that place, Marguerite stacked them to close off the opening as best she could to keep away wolves and foxes. There was nothing she could do about mink and weasels, and she would not think about them chewing on his meagre flesh.

"How did he die?"

"He lost hope."

"Lost hope?"

"Did he not have cause?"

"There is always faith, Marguerite, always hope," Thevet says gravely. "Even in the darkest night." He would admonish me with the same platitudes Marguerite tried so fervently to believe.

La fille naïve. Foolish girl. Km-mm-mm. Saved by our grace, not God's.

"*Oui*," I answer.

While the Franciscan rambles on about faith, I stare at the stone wall behind him. I see Michel's haunted eyes, glinting, but not with love. Even before he died, love had become a hazy memory for Marguerite, some wondrous thing that had happened to someone else in some distant time. Even when he lay beside her, she could no longer even imagine love. She could imagine only food, and when she dreamed it was of tables groaning with platters of roast pork, beef, and goose, golden loaves of bread, sweet butter, almonds, and fruit tarts. She woke to the granite walls of the cave, to the dry bones they boiled for broth.

The days began to lengthen but were still bitterly cold, the winds so fierce Marguerite's eyelashes froze together and she could hardly breathe. Often in the morning she had to clear away snow from the cave's entrance, then her eyes would ache from the sun's brilliance. Michel now left the cave only to relieve himself, so Marguerite had to learn how to set snares and to hunt with the arquebus and fusil, though the large musket's recoil sometimes knocked her to the ground and bruised her shoulder.

She had long given up trying to poison the tenacious child within, but she still dug roots and stripped the inner bark from birch and alder to boil for broth. She used the axe to chop holes in the ice of the ponds so that she could fish and Damienne could dip water.

By late winter the rabbits and partridge were starving as well. They were scrawny with no fat at all. Marguerite saw no more deer tracks, but occasionally they ate a wolf she had managed to shoot from the entrance of the cave. In her dreams then, she would see wolves feeding on their bodies, ripping the baby from her belly, and tearing it apart. She would wake terrified and weary, as if she had not slept at all.

They became skeletal, and Marguerite could not comprehend how her belly could swell even as her arms and legs wasted away, how the child could kick and be so alive when she was dying. In half thoughts that drifted and meandered with the smoke from the fire, Marguerite came to believe that God was punishing them all for her sin, not for the sin of loving Michel, but for the sin of not wanting her baby.

O Lord, rebuke me not in thy indignation, nor chastise me in thy wrath. Have mercy on me...Praise the Lord, for he is good, for his mercy endureth for ever.

"Foolish, foolish girl," I say.

"We must never–" The Franciscan stops mid-sentence. "What? What did you say?" He waves a quill as if the words he seeks are hanging in the air between us and the feather might gather them in. "What did you say?" he repeats.

"Foolish."

"*Oui*, your young man was foolish. Tell me, how did he really die?"

"He died because God did not hear her prayers. Or because he chose not to answer."

Now the quill points. "Blasphemy," he shouts. "Take care what you say."

"Or what?" I feel a smile pull at the corners of my mouth. "Would you have me executed here – in the stronghold of the Huguenots? Or would you take me back to Paris?"

"Impertinent wench," he spits. "Tell me, how did he die?"

"Hopelessness, *Père*. I told you, he died of hopelessness."

Marguerite came to fear the man whom only seven months earlier she had loved with every part of her being. Michel's dark curls had dulled and thinned, and his beard was matted and filthy. His gums bled and his front teeth had fallen out. Michel's face looked like a skull, grinning hideously, even though he never smiled. Marguerite could no longer bear to look at him. His countenance repulsed her, and his glinting eyes frightened her. He had begun grumbling incoherently about Roberval, about demons and the Devil, about dying like mongrels, eyes picked by ravens. His words, rarely intelligible, descended to a growling monotone.

Marguerite took Michel's dagger and kept it close at hand. She began to sleep only when he slept and always left Damienne armed with the sabre.

One day when Marguerite returned from hunting

with only a few frozen berries to show for her efforts, she knew that something had changed. As soon as she entered the cave she could smell it. Death, the dusty scent entwined with grey smoke. When her eyes adjusted to the cave's perpetual darkness, she saw Damienne huddled against the wall, staring at Michel, who lay sprawled on his back, toothless mouth grinning.

Marguerite knelt in front of Damienne. What happened? she said.

Damienne looked over Marguerite's shoulder, to Michel. They have come, she said.

Who has come?

The demons. They came for him.

Non, that cannot be! Marguerite pushed herself away from the old woman.

He began talking to them, Damienne said.

Talking to them?

Oui, he talked and laughed with them. But it was not a good laughter. His eyes glowed just like a wolf's. He reached out to them and they took him.

It must have been angels, said Marguerite. Michel is at peace now. He's in heaven.

Non. I saw them. Uncountable. Like black smoke.

Marguerite grabbed for her New Testament and held it to her chest. Angels, she insisted, they must have been angels.

Non, whispered Damienne. They were not.

A sliver of icy doubt slipped into Marguerite's heart. She did not really believe that angels had come for Michel, but she could not, would not, believe that demons had been in the cave. Michel and Damienne had conjured them from their own fear.

Marguerite knelt and gathered Michel into her arms. She tried to feel grief but could manage only a profound weariness. And anger. Why had he given up? Why would he not fight to live long enough to see his child?

"Hopelessness does not kill," Thevet protests. "How did he die?"

L'homme faible. Weak. Weak. Weak. Km-mm-mm.

"Oh, but it does, *Père*, it does."

"But you lived. Damienne lived."

L'homme faible. Kek-kek-kek. L'homme faible.

"Her husband was a good man, but weak. He lost hope, and then the angels came."

"Angels?" The Franciscan's face brightens.

"*Oui*, angels."

My belly is hollow, and blood pulses across that painful emptiness. I am carrying a brace of rabbits, gutted but not yet skinned. The fur is soft in my hand as I run up the stairs, two at a time, and into the garret. I cannot wait. I rip the skin from the meat and bite into cold grey flesh. I chew until I can close my eyes and breathe. I swallow, then bite again. I look up and see the striped cat. She does not move. She is watching me from the open window. I see now what she sees: my teeth sunk into raw meat, eyes savage.

I pull the rabbit away from my mouth. The cat turns and flees.

I set the rabbits aside and kindle a fire in the hearth. I will use the iron pot, cook the rabbits into a stew, and put the stew on a plate with bread.

I sit by the fire, my hunger satisfied for now. I have even left a small portion of stew outside the window. Now and again I turn from the hearth to see if the cat has come back. Why do I care? She is scrawny and ugly, her ear tattered, and she would bite me if she could. There is no mercy in her green eyes.

But I have seen her distended belly, and I worry. She is starving. She might eat them. I cannot let her eat them. And so I keep watch.

The spider spins, patient and painstaking in her weaving. She listens more attentively than the Franciscan, and I decide to offer her something beautifu: a butterfly. The spider is sated now, so the butterfly is safe. I see the flash of iridescent wings.

Marguerite began wearing Michel's clothes. She tied his breeches with hemp rope below her swollen belly and tugged his soldier's thick doublet onto her shoulders and across her chest. She held the cloth to her nose and breathed in the scent of his skin – salt and berries – still lingering beneath the stink of sweat and fear. She pulled on his long wool stockings and stuffed dry grass into his boots to make them fit.

She willed herself to forget what he had become and to remember only what he had been. Marguerite began to think of Michel with love and tenderness, recalling how he had spoken with joyful expectation about children – *our many, many children* – and how she would teach them letters and numbers, teach them with books brought from France. It was as if she could carry him gently within her, shaping him to fit within the spaces in her heart the way she had shaped his clothes to fit her body. She could remember now how he'd held her close, how he'd touched her with his fingertips and tongue. She could close her eyes and see his smile. She could see love now, and not anger and despair, in the golden flecks of his jade eyes.

L'amour. L'espoir. La fille naïve.

"*Oui*," I answer. "She was foolish to love, foolish to hope."

The spider lifts a leg, testing the air. Perhaps she too hears the voices. I direct my question to her. "But what else could she do?"

One morning, about ten days after she had buried Michel, Marguerite emerged from the cave to see the ice beyond the large islands littered with dark spots. Sabre in hand, she walked slowly down to the harbour and across the ice, approaching cautiously. As she crept closer, the crying bleats became deafening, and the spots resolved into seals – scores of small white pups accompanied by grey adults whose dark markings meandered across their shoulders and backs.

Her stride ungainly, Marguerite had to stretch across a narrow vein of open water to reach the floe upon which they rested. Though the seals seemed only mildly wary of her approach, she watched them closely, her stomach roused to hunger, the baby kicking hard in anticipation. Finally she saw a small one, bleating, apparently alone and unguarded. Marguerite crept closer, raised the sabre, and stabbed. Again and again, in a frenzy, she stabbed the writhing body so that the seal stained its white fur with its own red blood. When the pup lay still, she gutted it at once and ate the liver, hot and steaming.

Curious black faces turned and watched, but did not threaten.

Though small, the seal pup was heavy, and Marguerite strained to move it. As if her baby understood, it lay still and quiet. Marguerite, strengthened by food, managed to lift the seal across the vein of open water and then tug and slide it toward shore. She carried it to the cave like an offering, every muscle aching with exhaustion.

Roused from emaciated lethargy, Damienne was ecstatic. She quickly ate the heart, though it hurt her teeth, which had loosened in her swollen gums. She licked crimson blood from her lips and grinned.

Using the sabre, the axe, and Michel's dagger, they stripped the seal of its heavy white fur, cut the body into pieces and carried them into the cave. Their stomachs rumbled as they watched and smelled the roasting meat, fat dripping and sizzling in the fire. Unable to wait for the dark meat to cook fully,

Marguerite and Damienne ate until they were glutted and drowsy.

Eyes heavy, Marguerite stared into the fire, not quite believing their good fortune. She rubbed her swollen belly and murmured psalms of praise: I will love thee, O Lord, my strength. The Lord is my firmament, my refuge, and my deliverer. My God is my helper, and in him will I put my trust...And they cried to the Lord in their tribulation, and he delivered them out of their distresses.

Marguerite praised and thanked God, but believed it was Michel who had brought her – and the baby – this gift of food. Her love for him, and her grief, grew larger.

She slept then, but fitfully. Marguerite fretted, anxious for the dawn, fearing the seals would be gone before morning. Then she worried that the baby would come too soon, that she would be too weak to hunt. She put her hands on her belly and whispered, Wait, child. Wait. Let me hunt, let me find food.

Marguerite agonized over how they could preserve the meat. They had no salt. How could they dry it and yet keep the wolves away? She wondered how she could tan the heavy white furs to make cloaks and boots.

Très inquiète. Km-mm-mm.

"*Oui*," I answer. "She worried. Always she worried."

Marguerite was granted nearly a fortnight to kill seals. She and Damienne ate as much as they could, then they rendered the fat, saving the oil in the seals' own stomachs and bladders. They cut the meat into thin strips they could dry outside during the day. At dusk they laboured to move everything into the cave to keep it away from the wolves, foxes, and weasels.

Then, crystallizing out of white fog, the white bears came. Enormous and ferocious.

I hear again the *huff-huff-huff* just outside the cave and see a huge white paw snaking in between the rocks and pulling at the wooden barriers. I tell the spider about the bears and about Marguerite's terror. Lifting her front legs, she captures my words and wraps them tightly in her silky thread, confining the memories – and the fear – within her web.

Isabelle leaves her bench and sidles closer. She shows me her slate, the letters neat and carefully formed. She has drawn a small bird in the corner. Each foot has five crooked toes. "Do you think God is too busy sometimes?" she asks.

"Too busy?"

"Papa says that maybe God was so busy with the king's wars that he couldn't hear my prayers for Mama." Her voice is small and quiet, words lisped through the gap in her front teeth. "And that's why she died." Isabelle waits, wanting an affirmation – or a denial. There is anger within her, but a great sorrow beneath.

How long, O Lord, wilt thou forget me? How long? Deaf to her prayers.

She sighs loudly, then tucks her slate under her arm and returns to her bench. She knows her letters are well-formed and that I have no answer.

"The Indians there live almost exclusively on fish, especially seals, whose flesh is very good and delicate to them," says the Franciscan. "And they make an oil from the fat, which, when melted, is a reddish colour. They drink it with their meals as we would drink wine or water. They make coats and clothing from its skin."

Has Thevet forgotten already that he told me all of this only three days ago?

"The seals," he says, "tell me more about the seals."

"They brought the bears."

"Bears!" Thevet sits up in his chair. "What kind of bears?"

"Huge white ones." Bears larger than any animal Marguerite had ever seen, and all the more terrifying because they rose up suddenly where only moments before there had been only white fog, snow, and ice. There was ferocity in their small black eyes, a savagery she could see whenever a bear attacked a seal, smashing its head with a single swipe of an enormous paw.

White on white on white. Scarlet blood the only colour. And then *kek-kek-kek, pruk-pruk-pruk.* Ebony wings iridescent with a violet sheen.

I look behind the monk and see a shaggy paw poke out from between the stones. The long yellow claws nearly touch his head. Then the paw is withdrawn, replaced by a white snout. *Huff-huff-huff*. I smell the stink of rancid seal meat.

"With your lover dead, how did you protect yourselves?"

"Marguerite killed four in one day. With a musket."

"Four! In one day?" He scribbles furiously.

L'idiot, filling his costly paper with nonsense. No one could kill four bears in one day. Thirteen steps to load and shoot an arquebus, a fire-steel at hand to light the fuse, the powder unreliable. One shot, no time to reload and fire before the bear smashes your skull as easily as a seal's.

In the dark, their eyes shining a silvery blue, Marguerite shot at them, but only to keep them away from the cave. Marguerite and Damienne were forced to dry whatever seal meat they could, and to smoke it, within the cave, even during the day. After the bears came, Marguerite went outside only for water and wood. Damienne would venture out only to relieve herself, and then she would not go far. The old woman not only feared the bears, she had also begun to see demons in every shadow.

Thevet sits back and studies me, wary now of a woman who can kill bears. "Great with child, but hunting bears." He shakes his head, incredulous.

"They ate them," I say, enlarging upon my story. "The meat was tough and tasted of fish. They used the furs for blankets."

He writes more slowly now, perhaps uncertain he can believe me. "And when was the infant born?"

"The tenth day of April in 1543. Two hundred and seventy-two days after Roberval left them." Damienne's hands fluttering with every scream. Alertness dimming, fading, brought back to herself by pain. Agonizing pain ripping through her belly. Blood.

"Girl or boy."

"It does not matter." I rub the cut on my wrist, nearly healed now, but I can still make it hurt. I watch his mouth move, but hear only the buzzing within my head. Finally, I hear him. Then wish for deafness.

"Of course it matters," he says. "He, or she, was the grandchild of nobles."

Outside the window, dogs begin fighting. Low growls and yips. I think of wolves, copper eyes and flash of teeth, and hear them lurking just beyond the door, the swish of tails against wood, click of nails on stone.

The Franciscan flinches at each snarl, but persists in his questions. "Tell me more about the child. How did you manage to bear the child alone?"

"She was not alone. Her servant Damienne was there...*oui*, Damienne." I say the name twice to make him think of her, twice to annoy him. I say it again. "Damienne was there."

Thevet runs his tongue over his teeth, but refrains from calling her names.

Damienne, almost no help at all, her moans and whines as pitiful and fearful as the dogs' outside.

"Marguerite had been eating seal meat," I say. "She was strong."

Thevet pounces on the word seal, and I sit and listen – for a third time – to what the monk has already told me. "The Indians of Terre Neuve live almost exclusively on seals," he says importantly, as if imparting new knowledge. "They make a reddish oil from the fat." He stops and blinks, perhaps remembering now that he was asking about the baby, not seals. "Were you within the cave?"

I nod. Dark walls. Smoke. Flames reaching high, receding, a sacred rite as old as Eve.

"Was it painful?"

I know what the Franciscan wants to hear: Eve banished from the garden to bear her children in pain because of her sin of disobedience.

"Would it not be sin if it were not?" My words are brittle.

Marguerite's thoughts were broken threads, weaving in and out of pain and fear, ends fraying, wet with blood. She floated above, watching and listening, and heard voices that were neither hers nor Damienne's, one weak and rasping like Michel's, another low and harsh like Roberval's. Their words accused her: *Lascivious coquette. Le désir. Scandal. Whore. Punished. Le bâtard misérable. Le bâtard, le bâtard, le bâtard.*

Non, non, non, she screamed, my baby is not a bastard! In defiance, she pushed the child out – a howling infant, her face screwed up in rage at having been born in such a place. Marguerite used Michel's dagger to cut the cord. The voices stilled.

"Marguerite pushed until her *womb* was empty."

"Stop!" Thevet's hand jerks and papers spill to the floor. The monk pretends outrage that I would say such a word aloud in his presence. He gathers the papers, then sits and glares until his breathing slows.

"Boy or girl?" he says pointedly. "You must tell me, Marguerite. He, or she, was the grandchild of nobles."

"Perhaps not, *Père*. Perhaps everything I've told you is wrong. Perhaps Marguerite coupled with one of the prisoners, a murderer, and gave birth to a bastard."

"You are shameless," he hisses. "Just like the Whore of Babylon with your carnal abominations, your insatiable desires."

Les abominations charnelles. Kek-kek-kek. Les désirs insatiables.

I touch the blade of Michel's dagger. If I could cut the cords that bind my throat, I would laugh in his face. The Franciscan has no idea how insatiable I am, how much I hunger for blood.

Thevet considers me, his yellow-brown eyes filled with disdain. He shakes his head slowly, pretending at pity. "Even after all these years, and Roberval's punishment, you remain unrepentant for all you have done."

La culpabilité. Huff-huff-huff. Grievous sin. Kek-kek-kek. Impardonnable. The voices are tangled, tripping one upon the other: *La contrition et la pénitence. Km-mm-mm. Le bâtard, le bâtard, le bâtard.*

"What was the child's name, Marguerite? We will stay here until you tell me."

I put my hands over my ears. I will not give him contrition. I will not give him penitence. And I will not give him a name.

The Franciscan picks up a knife and sharpens a quill with quick angry strokes. He throws the quill down. He has cut off the nib and spoiled it. He picks up another.

Marguerite called her Michella: gift from God. She put the infant to her breast and prayed there would be enough milk. She and Damienne had not prepared for a baby. They had not believed it possible that Marguerite could birth a living child – or that the child could survive its birth. They now marvelled at this miracle, at Michella's beauty and her strength, the satiny smoothness of her skin, the vigour with which she sucked, fighting to live.

Marguerite refused to remember that she had ever tried to poison this child, that she had ever wished her baby dead. She now set her mind upon the Holy Virgin and her child, knowing she would do anything to save Michella. Anything.

Damienne tore up their tattered undershifts for rags. After a few weeks, when the seals and bears were gone and the snow had melted away from the bogs, the old woman found the courage to venture forth to collect moss that she dried in the warm sun.

Michella revived their hope and their faith.

Be thou unto me a God, a protector, and a house of refuge, to save me. Have mercy upon us...mercy upon us...mercy upon us. Kek-kek-kek.

I hear Michella's whimpers, loud then soft. I feel pain in the centre of my chest. I press the wound at my wrist, then hear the whispers: *Être indulgent, c'est mourir.*

"*Oui*," I answer quietly, talking down into my lap. "To be soft is to die."

The monk does not look up from his quill and his knife.

With the thawing of the ice and the arrival of warm weather, Marguerite was convinced, now more than ever, that Roberval would finally send a ship. When he looked upon Michella, he would forgive them.

But could she forgive her uncle for Michel's death? Marguerite saw again the hopelessness and desperation in Michel's face. Why did he not fight to live? Even to see his daughter, to protect her?

The knife clicks, then scrapes, a repeated whisper: *le bâtard misérable, le bâtard misérable.*

"*Non*, not a bastard," I answer.

Thevet looks up. "So the child was not a bastard."

"*Non*, it was not."

I stand to leave.

"We are not yet done."

"I am done. You have asked, and I have told you: Marguerite birthed a child. The child lived."

"But the name...what was the name?"

I turn away and open the door to face the wolves. Michella, Michella, Michella, I say to them in my head. They snarl, then scatter.

It is nearly dawn and I have not slept. Yet, I have dreamed. In the glowing embers, I see his face, ravaged by pox, mouth filled with dark rotted stubs. The stench of his black breath still hangs in the air.

He came to me weeks ago, or perhaps it was months, or years. Perhaps he never came at all, except in my dreams.

Marguerite had seen him flogged aboard the *Vallentyne*. A felon released to Roberval for his colony, the man survived Charlesbourg Royal and returned to France a free man. He managed, somehow, to find me, the woman he believed to be Marguerite. He accosted me in the schoolroom downstairs, just after the girls had left, as if he had been waiting and watching just outside the scrivener's shop. I protested but could not dissuade him from his conviction that I was Marguerite. When I tried to leave, he followed me up the stairs, hopping along behind me on his good leg and using his stiff leg like a crutch. Hop-scrape, hop-scrape. I stopped on the stairs so he would not force his way into my room.

There was no gold or silver or precious jewels in New France, the man said bitterly, and when winter came and food was scarce, Roberval had us flogged for being hungry...or for lechery or buggery or bestiality. The man laughed darkly. He punished us for sins only the viceroy himself could imagine.

The man shrugged his shoulders over and over again and winced as if the wounds on his back still bled and burned. He spat the name when he told me that Roberval had hanged six of the colonists. For disobedience, he said. Their bodies hung for days as a warning to us all.

When I stared into his scarred face, I could see their legs kicking, their bodies stiff and swaying, turning black in the wind and cold.

The man leaned close and whispered, his breath rank and his spittle spraying my cheek. I was there, he said, when he put you ashore. He folded his hands delicately under his chin. And the cowardly noblemen and soldiers stood aside, he said, like faint-hearted ladies. He dropped his hands to his crotch and cupped it in imitation of the hapless nobles. Or men with no balls, he hissed.

How you must hate your uncle, he continued. He cocked his head and gave me a sidelong look before he spoke again. Roberval is often in Paris, at court, the cousin of King Henri's whore. He put his hands to his chest as if he were fondling breasts and gave me a lecherous grin.

He extended his grimy hand and rubbed his thumb against his first two fingers. For very little, he said, I could make your uncle pay for what he did...to all of us.

I did not trust him. He would take my money and do nothing. Yet I remember an open palm, coins gleaming, gold and silver. Did I give him money?

I have no gold or silver.

I can see so clearly the ice-blue eyes and the gaping wound beneath the square jaw. I can hear the rush of air from the severed windpipe and see scarlet blood dripping from the blade of Michel's dagger.

I raise a hand to my nose. My fingers smell as if I have been butchering a seal.

Did I only will it so? Can willing something make it happen?

Isabelle hums to herself as she studies a Latin grammar. The book is precious, our only copy, and she is not permitted to touch it. I turn the vellum pages for her. Isabelle is too young to learn Latin, and yet I am oddly pleased that she is eager to learn the language of scholars.

"*Amo, amas, amant,*" she reads, then looks to me for affirmation. I nod.

I watch Isabelle's lips, so like Michel's, and Michella's. Her skin is soft, translucent and glowing. I want to lean close and bury my face in her dark curls.

Before her birth, Michella had fed gluttonously on seal meat and fat. She was born plump and white, like a seal pup, and just as loud, bawling and mewling for her mother's milk. Marguerite too had fed heavily on seals – Michel's gift to them – so that her breasts filled with sweet milk that was rich with fat.

She and Damienne had managed to preserve enough seal meat and oil to remain within the cave – and safe from bears – for several weeks after Michella's birth, until after the seals and bears were gone. When open water appeared near shore, masses of ducks and geese descended. Hordes of seabirds nested on the rocky ledges on the western side of the island, setting up a terrible wonderful din. Even the clumsy Damienne could catch the birds with the twine net. Marguerite and Damienne were awed by the abundance.

Marguerite, her mouth craving something green and fresh, bound Michella to her chest with cloth torn from undershifts and went out to collect new shoots and leaves not yet unfurled. With bellies no longer painful with hunger, she and Damienne could stand and marvel at the enormous islands of ice that floated past: azure and green and aquamarine. The craggy islands appeared and then were gone within days. Marguerite and Damienne marvelled, but they prayed to see white sails, not mountains of ice. Marguerite prayed in both French and Latin.

La grâce de Dieu. Misericordia Deus.

God remained silent in both French and Latin. *Le silence. Silentium.*

I hear chuckling laughter, an infant's whimpers, then only Isabelle softly repeating the Latin words.

With the sea ice gone, and with it the wolves and fearsome bears, Marguerite and Damienne resumed building fires on the rocky beach near the harbour, piling them high with green boughs.

Roberval will come for us now, Marguerite assured Damienne, again and again. The old woman only nodded, and Marguerite said nothing about her fear that something dreadful had happened to her uncle and the ships.

Even if Roberval himself cannot come for us, she told Damienne, someone will. Surely.

Under bright daylight and with Michella at her breast, Marguerite read her New Testament and prayed. She continued marking the cave wall for each passing day, renewing the marks that had been blackened by smoke.

Her face serious, Isabelle nods for me to turn the page, unmindful of her beautiful lips murmuring words that are strange and foreign on her tongue. "*Esse, celere, ferre.*"

I want to lean in close and sniff her cheek. It would smell of violets and grass.

"*Habere*," she whispers.

Habere. To have, to hold.

Marguerite gazed in amazement at the child she held in her arms. How had this wondrous creature come to her? The greedy mouth at her breast was a source of both comfort and tortuous memory. Freed from the cave's darkness, the sun warm on her face, and her belly no longer screaming its hunger, Marguerite could remember love. She felt an empty ache that she had not felt for months, and she began to long for the Michel she'd known aboard ship and in their first few days on the island – Michel in the garden. She wanted to show him the baby she was certain now he would adore. She envisioned his dazzling smile, the golden flecks in his eyes. She yearned to make love in the grassy meadows, under the benevolent sun, a warm wind caressing them. The baby sucked, and Marguerite recalled his mouth on her breast, his hands on her hips, pulling her to him. She remembered, then she hugged Michella to her chest and wept.

"*Exspecto*," Isabelle says, "to expect, anticipate, hope for." She bows her head, then looks up at me through dark lashes. "Papa says I must hope for a wealthy husband, that I must be sinless...and hope. What do you hope for, Madame de Roberval?"

Her question startles me. Hope. What do I hope for?

"*Nihilum*," I answer. "I hope for nothing."

Isabelle's smooth brow furrows. Her grey eyes hold questions she does not know how to ask. She is too young. Like Marguerite, she cannot understand how someone can hope for nothing.

Marguerite was out collecting eggs from the nests of seabirds, Michella bound to her chest, when broad white sails came into view. Thinking at first that her eyes, and her mind, were deceiving her, she stood and watched. Then, heart pounding wildly, she ran down to the harbour and threw wood and green boughs onto the fire to build it as high as she could. Thick smoke billowed heavenward, carrying with it her most fervent prayers: My hope is in my God...O save me for thy mercy's sake...The Lord is my firmament, my refuge, and my deliverer...My deliverer, my deliverer, my deliverer...For thy mercy's sake, save us, save us, save us.

Marguerite jumped up and down, flailing her arms, then hurried to the cave. She gave Michella to Damienne, grabbed her rose silk gown from the trunk, and ran back down to the harbour. She tied the gown to a stout stick and waved it in wide arcs. She waved her pink flag until her arms and shoulders ached and she could no longer hold the stick aloft.

The ship came closer. Marguerite could see from its flags that it was not Roberval's, nor even a French ship. It was Portuguese. The ship passed by slowly, then sailed away.

Shoulders shaking with her sobs, Marguerite stared at the receding sails through a blur of tears. Why had God offered hope only to snatch it away? She slumped down to the rocks. Why?

She sat until long after the sun had set, shredding the silk gown. As her fingers worked, she tried to set her thoughts upon Job, God's beloved but tested servant. Job's trials were designed by the Devil, not God.

Marguerite released the fluttering strips of silk to the wind.

"*Nihilum*," Isabelle repeats. "Nothing."

I nod, pleased with how quickly she learns.

I have gorged on bread. On the island there was no bread after the hard biscuit was gone, and no grain, just a few seeds Marguerite could boil into a thin gruel. Nothing to grind for flour. I can stand for hours now rubbing my fingertips through flour, sometimes silky, sometimes coarse, redolent of wheat, barley, oats, and rye.

I cannot get enough bread, and when I manage to save a few coins, I hurry to the baker's. I was there before dawn this morning, and even before I was out his door, I began tearing off chunks of the warm loaf and stuffing them into my mouth. The whole loaf was gone by the time I returned to the garret, and now I have nothing.

The striped cat was there, just outside the window. I reached out to her, slowly, but she turned and ran, bouncing away on her pirate's leg.

I looked in the iron pot, but it was empty. I had no food to offer her, not even a scrap of stew or a bit of old cheese. She is starving.

I walk in circles. I cannot sit.

The iron pot. Why did I bring it back? Before the Franciscan came – probing, prodding, poking at me with questions as sharp as a pointed beak – I used it, and the pot was only a pot. Now I cannot touch it without remembering the island. The pot held everything: water, stewed rabbit, deer, duck, gull, and seal, fish and mussels and whelks, eggs, the rendered fat from seals and whales, gruel and berries, weasel, wolf, and mink, leaves and roots, seaweed and the inner bark of birch and willow boiled for broth. Dry bones, shells, and strips of hide boiled until the water remained clear. Everything.

In the early summer, Marguerite and Damienne gorged on half a dozen different kinds of seabirds and their eggs. Fish became more plentiful and easier to catch.

Marguerite reached her arms to the sky: manna from heaven. God in his mercy.

The whales followed, the sea exploding with their spray. Damienne, believing them to be monsters, shuddered each time their broad backs and tails breached the water. Marguerite could only hope that one of the huge beasts would strand itself upon the rocks.

Marguerite had milk and Michella thrived. Damienne would sit with her in the warm sun and sing lullabies.

I close my eyes and hear the soft notes of the old woman's voice: *Chut, petite bébé, je t'aime, je t'aime.* I hear a baby's coos and babbles, and I smile. Then I hear wails fade to whimpers fade to silence.

I would weep, but Marguerite shed all of our tears. There are none left for me. I reach for the dagger and make small cuts along my wrist. A voice counts: *un, deux, trois, quartre, cinq.*

I dab at the blood with the black hem of my skirt, already crusted with mud.

The days lengthened, then began to shorten again. Marguerite and Damienne kept a fire burning near the harbour. Now and again they saw white sails in the distance.

Surely, Marguerite thought, the sailors and fishermen saw their smoke. Why would they not come near? She began to wonder if the fishermen believed the fires were kindled by Indians – or by demons – set to lure them to their deaths.

With every ship that passed and did not stop, Damienne's face grew more haggard, her shoulders more stooped. Marguerite could not set aside her concern that tragedy had befallen the colony, that

Indians had killed the colonists, or that the ships had
sunk and her uncle was dead. She convinced herself,
again and again, and tried her best to convince
Damienne that, were he alive, Roberval would come
for them.

Foolish girl. Le cœur noir de Roberval.

"*Oui,*" I answer, "foolish to trust Roberval's
black heart."

Still, Marguerite hoped, and she prayed that a
ship would come: Have mercy on me, and hear my
prayer.

Foolish hope, foolish prayers. Chuckling laughter,
muffled pounding.

I pull my hands from my ears. Someone is knocking. I crack open the door, and there is Isabelle, her
small fist still raised. I have forgotten the girls.

"Madame de Roberval–"

"Go, I'll be down in a moment." I slam the door
in her face, then smooth my skirts and wind my hair
into a tight chignon at the back of my neck. I have
given no thought as to what I will teach them today.
But it matters little what they know – and what they
do not. Their lives will not be of their own choosing.
And the more money their fathers have for dowries,
the less choice they will have.

Choice. Roberval gave her none. But Marguerite
took it. She chose, and for three months, she loved
boldly and outrageously. Love. She gave it, and she
took it. Until Michel scorned her.

*L'amour. Le désir. La demoiselle déshonorante.
La putain misérable.*

"Stop!" I scream. "She was not a whore."

The voices follow me down the stairs: *Le comportement scandaleux. La perversité. Murderer.*

I stop on the last stair. "She was not a murderer. Nor am I."

La culpabilité. Grievous sin. Debts must be paid.

I lean against the wall to catch my breath. "She meant only to save her baby," I gasp. "And she paid her debt. Marguerite paid."

When I enter the room, the girls' heads are bowed. Only Isabelle looks up, her face eager. She does not yet know what lies ahead. She does not yet know that she will be given no choice, that she is far too intelligent ever to be happy with what her father and her husband will choose for her.

I tell the girls to continue practising their darning. Isabelle screws up her face. Instead of picking up her needle and yarn and her frayed stocking with its knots and lumps, she comes forward and tugs on my hand. Her face is alarmed when she sees the angry scabs, and I pull my sleeve down over my wrist.

"Madame de Roberval," she says, "for last night's lesson, Papa read from the Bible about Abraham and Isaac...about obedience to God." She hesitates and chooses her words carefully. "Abraham was going to kill his own son," she says incredulously.

When Isabelle speaks again, her voice is soft, as if she is telling me a secret. "I asked Papa why God would want that, but he shushed me. He told me to listen...and then I would understand. Do you understand?"

"Understand what?"

"Why God would ask you to do something bad."

I try not to hear the low growls: *L'obéissance. Obedientia. God's will. Km-mm-mm.*

"We must obey God," I say carefully, "as you would obey your father. And do whatever he asks of you."

"Even if God asks you to kill someone?"

"Even then."

"But what if he doesn't stop you?"

"Even then, Isabelle."

Putting a finger to her chin, she looks up and to the side, face puzzled. "But how do you know the voice you hear is not the Devil pretending to be God?"

The voices hum: *La voix de Dieu, la voix du Diable. Km-mm-mm. Kek-kek-kek. Murderer. Grievous sin. Impardonnable.*

"One just knows," I hear myself say. "Get your stocking, Isabelle. You should practise."

"But–"

"Go!"

Pouting, she turns away.

I want to grab her shoulders and spin her around. I want to say: How we know, Isabelle, is that God never speaks. It was Abraham who stopped his hand from killing his son. Not God.

"There was food in the summer: seabirds and eggs, fish, berries, mussels," I say, answering questions I have answered before. "Huge fish moved into the streams. Marguerite used the spear. They smoked and dried the flesh. She found a small whale washed up on shore." I am out of breath from having said so much.

"What about the child? How did you care for the child?"

"Marguerite had milk, at least through the summer. She wrapped the baby in rabbit skins, in the white pelts of seals."

"Not unlike *les sauvages*," Thevet says thoughtfully. He raises a finger and stares upward. "As to the treatment of babies, they are clever. They wrap them up in four or five marten skins sewn together, then tie them to a plank with a hole through it." He uses his hands and his quill to draw in the air, as if he has seen all this himself. "Between the legs is a sort of spout made of soft bark where the infant can make water without soiling its body or the furs." He looks at me – his audience – and smiles. "Clever, *non*?"

His thoughts circle back to Marguerite. "If you had food," he says, "why did the old woman die?" He cannot bring himself to say her name.

"They had food for the summer, but it was more than a year before the Breton ship came to the island."

"I understand that. But what happened that fall?" The monk understands nothing.

"Too much. Not enough." I ball my hands into fists. My nails dig into my palms. I push them in harder. It is a pain I know how to feel.

Thevet gives an irritated snap of his thick fingers, as if to bring me back from someplace distant. "Do not speak to me in riddles," he says. "What happened?"

"They baptised the baby."

"And what did you use for holy water, for consecrated oil and salt?"

"The sea and seal oil. All blessed by God."

"And the baptismal name?" he asks, ignoring my sarcasm.

I stare down at my hands and hear his annoyed sigh.

"When did the old bawd die?"

"Damienne," I say loudly, "died on the fourth day of November in 1543." Scrape of stone upon stone. "Four hundred and eighty days after Roberval left them."

"How?" He does not look up from his scribbling.

"She slipped and fell from a cliff." I release myself to float above, gliding on raven's wings. I fix my eyes on the candles and quills so I will not see the images that come in my dreams. White bone. Eye to bloody sky.

I read the words he has written: *Damienne, November, cliff, baptised.*

With every ship that passed and did not stop, Damienne's eyes grew more distant, peering in, not out, and more faded, as if her soul were slowly leaking away. Both of them knew that after October no ship would come until spring, and perhaps not even then.

Was this to be their life? Michella's life? Only the three of them? Forever?

They had stores of food from the summer's bounty: smoked fish and berries, dried meat and rendered fat. But as the days grew shorter and colder, Damienne withered, her skin thin and jaundiced, stretched like parchment over knobby bones and swollen joints. She continued to help Marguerite with Michella, but the child no longer brought smiles.

Damienne stopped singing, and talking – except to herself.

After the birth of Michella, Damienne's sightings of demons had diminished, but as the days shortened she began seeing them everywhere: in the crevices of cliffs, behind rocks and trees, floating in the depths of dark pools. Like Michel, Damienne began mumbling about the Devil and death.

They will come for us, she would mutter, and the ravens will clean the flesh from our bones and pick out our eyes. She looked at Marguerite and snarled, Your desire, your sin, your guilt.

Damienne's eyes, like Michel's, took on a strange glint that made Marguerite afraid to leave Michella alone with her.

"What was the old woman doing up on the cliffs?"

From above, I watch my mouth move. "Picking berries."

"In November?"

"*Oui.*"

There were no berries on the cliffs. The sun was

setting when Marguerite saw Damienne fall. Or jump. Black silhouette against red sky. Too late. Too late. Damienne plummeted to the rocks and trees below before Marguerite could take three steps toward the bottom of the cliffs. The old woman's face was smashed beyond all recognition. But in my dreams, Damienne's skirts balloon out, and she drifts like a feather. Her face glows and her lips move, but I cannot hear her words as I scramble toward her, each step mired in mud, branches tangling around my ankles and tripping me. I hear only mocking voices: *Grievous sin, impardonnable. La culpabilité.* And then: *Un cadeau, un cadeau, un cadeau. A gift, a gift, a gift.*

I am always too late to catch her.

Staring toward the bloody sky, her dead eye accuses me. *Non, non,* I say in the dream, Marguerite's sin. It was Marguerite, not me.

I float now, watching. "She left Marguerite alone with the baby," I hear myself say to the monk.

Too agitated to sit, I pace, my fingers drumming, drumming, drumming against my thigh.

Marguerite had seen what she should not have seen, and she stood, unmoving. Lot's wife. A pillar of salt. She wasn't sad or frightened. She was furious. And envious. Had she not had Michella, she would have gone up on the cliff and thrown herself down beside Damienne.

Marguerite and Michella. Alone. No voice but her own.

The blood-red sky darkened to black, and the trees and rocks bled into the sea. The sun rose on a world drained of all colour – a white disk in a white sky over a white sea.

For days Marguerite heard nothing, as if she were surrounded by dense fog that muffled all sound. She refused to fashion a shroud or to search for a burial crypt. She would not read her New Testament over the corpse, nor would she pray or weep. She allowed the broken body to lie until it was no longer Damienne, until the accusing eye had been picked out and the carcass resembled a half-frozen seal washed up on shore, the flesh grey and cold. She left the body and the blood for the ravens, *un cadeau*, a gift.

Kek-kek-kek. La nourriture pour les corbeaux. Pruk-pruk-pruk.

"And why should the ravens not eat?" I look at my fingers, raven's claws. I am one of them now, dressed all in black.

My head hums with the sound of maggots gnawing. I rub my wrist and am surprised to touch scabbed flesh. Who has done this to me? Who has hurt me?

I collapse onto the bench and pull a blanket around me, the scratchy wool a comfort. The spider still labours among the logs, diligent, persistent, even though she has had her supper: Damienne's maggots.

Grievous sin. Impardonnable. La culpabilité.

"*Non*," I answer. "Marguerite's sin, not mine."

The spider stitches one strand to another, setting her snare. She is still hungry, but I will not give her Michella's butterflies. Michella should have had butterflies, with wings of sapphires and emeralds set in gold filigree. I hear an infant's whimpers fade to silence.

Late November. Wind. Freezing rain. Snow. The stored food gone.

Marguerite had nothing but a few scrawny rabbits, gulls, and partridge, berries she'd gathered and dried, mussels and whelks, and a few fish she could hook or spear. Ignoring her own hunger and struggling not to swallow, Marguerite chewed bits of meat to make them soft, then tried to feed them to Michella, but the infant's summer plumpness waned as surely as the daylight. Marguerite's breasts flattened, and though Michella sucked and sucked, she howled her hunger until her own wailing wore her out and finally, she slept.

December. Only dried berries, a few fish and mussels, boiled seaweed and bark. Breasts flat, no longer containing even a drop of milk.

Marguerite held her New Testament over Michella and wept. She prayed: Out of the depths I have cried to thee, O Lord. How long? How long? Have mercy upon us. Help us, help us, help us.

Or let us die.

She considered, and prayed, then considered again. Marguerite set her mind on the Virgin and Child, on how she would do anything to save her baby. Anything. Finally, feeling as if she were no longer in her own body, she watched herself use Michel's dagger to cut pieces from the frozen carcass that was no longer Damienne. Marguerite closed her eyes when she saw herself place the flesh into the black pot, boil it, and offer the broth and softened pieces to Michella.

La culpabilité. Grievous sin. Impardonnable.

"Marguerite's sin. Not mine."

Michella swallowed, but she grew thinner and thinner until she was a tiny skeleton, her green eyes huge and staring, her bones as light and fragile as a bird's. She no longer howled, only whimpered, then slept, silently.

Le silence. La pénitence. Debts must be paid. Km-mm-mm.

"Marguerite's debt, not mine."

One morning Marguerite could not wake her. Michella: gift from God. God had reclaimed her.

God had found Marguerite unworthy.

Marguerite could hardly stand beneath the weight of her grief and her guilt. She washed Michella, kissed her face, then wrapped the small body in the white fur of a seal to keep her warm. As the sun set and the sky became a rose to match the colour of Michella's perfect lips, Marguerite rolled the rocks away from the crevice where she had placed Michel, now only bones, his fingers and toes gone. She touched his grinning mouth, his cheeks, the empty eyes, then laid Michella beside him.

She could not bear to think of weasels and mink gnawing on her baby's little bird bones. She crawled in beside Michella to protect her. Marguerite lay down beside her baby and her husband.

Forgive me, O Lord, she prayed. Forgive me. I meant only to save Michella.

A psalm came to her, and she murmured into the dark: Hear, O Lord, my prayer, and let my cry come to thee. Turn not thy face away from me...For my days are vanished like smoke, and my bones are grown dry like fuel for the fire...I am become like a pelican of the wilderness. I am like a night raven in the house.

It was I who awoke in the morning to the raucous calls of ravens interwoven with voices and laughter: *Quork-quork-quork. The grace and mercy of God. Kek-kek-kek. Saved by our grace, not God's. Km-mm-mm.*

The voices mocked, but they also spoke sweetly, their breath scented with cinnamon and cloves: *Marguerite is dead, but you must live, Marguerite. Her sin, not yours. Saved by our grace.*

I stood, looked upon Michel and Michella and Marguerite, then rolled the rocks into place to seal their crypt. I walked away from them all. I walked away from her grievous sin.

God had turned his back to Marguerite. I turned my back to God.

"O Lord, our Lord, how admirable is thy name in the whole earth. For thy magnificence is elevated above the heavens…" The girls stand in a row at the front of the room, reciting in Latin, their words mumbled and garbled. Isabelle's is the only voice that rings out, her words clear and confident. Though she is the youngest, the other girls follow her lead. Isabelle, even with her lisp, is the only one who can pronounce the Latin correctly.

"For I will behold thy heavens," they drone, "the works of thy fingers, the moon and the stars which thou hast founded. What is man that thou art mindful of him?"

The voices taunt: *What is man that thou art mindful of him? Le silence. Km-mm-mm. How long, O Lord? How long?*

I turn my back and try to ignore both the voices and the psalm.

"Thou hast made him a little less than the angels, thou hast crowned him with glory and honour."

Finished now, the girls shuffle to the shelf to pick up their embroidery hoops, needles, and thread. I hear small sighs and the rustle of skirts sliding onto benches.

Isabelle tugs at my hand. "Madame de Roberval," she says, "have you ever seen an angel?"

"An angel?" I want to laugh out loud, but cannot. "*Non*," I say. "Never."

"Papa says Mama's an angel now, that she's in heaven. I would like to see her. Where do you think heaven is?"

"I don't know."

"My baby brother killed her." Isabelle speaks

with the bluntness of children. "He was born dead. Never baptised. Do you think he's in heaven with her?"

"I know nothing of heaven, Isabelle. Go get your hoops and needles."

"Papa says he is." She stands on tiptoe and cups her hand to her mouth as if she would tell me a secret. She wants me to lean down. And I do – though I have no wish to know her secrets – or her father's. "I hope not," she confesses, "because I hate him." Her forehead creases in worry. "Does that make me wicked?"

Grievous sin. La perversité. Impardonnable.

I take a deep breath. "*Non*, you are not wicked. No matter what you wish for."

The Franciscan looks up from his papers. "Why did you not bury the old woman?"

Pourquoi? Why? La culpabilité.

I put my hands over my ears and stare into the flame of a candle. I see porcelain skin, rosebud lips, two tiny pearl teeth.

"Put your hands down and tell me why you did not bury her."

I drop my hands into my lap. "Marguerite saved all her strength for the baby."

"So you just left her for the animals?"

"The flesh was no longer Damienne's."

La perversité. Grievous sin.

"So her bones lie there yet?" He looks at me as if I were a leper.

"*Non*, they do not." Scattered by wolves and foxes. Ravens.

He shakes his head as if he will never understand. That is true. He will not.

"What happened after the old woman died?" he says finally.

"No food. Marguerite had no milk. The baby starved." Whimpers gone to silence. Bones fragile as a robin's.

"When?"

"The sixth day of December. Five hundred and twelve days after Roberval left them." Scrape of stone upon stone.

"Did you bury the child?"

"Marguerite buried the baby beside its father."

"How did you survive the winter if you had no food?"

"She didn't."

He stares at me, his mouth twitching. "What do you mean?"

"Marguerite died."

"Died?"

"She died. I lived."

"*Impossible*," he whispers. His eyes, no longer cold hard marble, are bright and soft with fear. "Is it demons that make you say such strange things?" he asks. "Did you make promises to the Devil?"

I hear them then, the papery rustling that grows

louder: *Eight hundred and thirty-two days and nights. Alone for three hundred and twenty. Why? Pourquoi? Kek-kek-kek. Quork-quork-quork.*

"*Non, Père*, no promises to the Devil, no demons."

Her sin, not yours. Saved by our grace, not God's.

"They are not uncommon in those heathen lands." He speaks slowly, trying to calm himself. "The Indians are often tormented by evil spirits." He pauses, then gestures deliberately as if trying to explain something difficult to a child. His own words comfort him. "When I used to travel in their country, *les sauvages* would come and throw themselves into my arms, shouting, 'the evil spirit is beating and tormenting me. Help me, I beg of you.'"

I sit, hands folded in my lap, and do not move.

"And immediately," he continues, "I would seize them and recite the Gospel of Saint John, which invariably delivered them from the evil spirit." He nods. "I performed this most holy and Catholic act more than one hundred times."

Thevet picks up a quill and tries to still his fingers' trembling, but the feather quivers in his hand. "I could do the same for you, Marguerite. There is no shame. Christ himself removed seven demons from Mary Magdalene and she became holy." He opens a Bible and begins reciting in Latin: "In the beginning was the Word, and the Word was with God, and the Word–"

I spring forward and bare my teeth. "*Non, Père*," I say. "I am not tormented by demons. I am tormented by you."

He shrinks back, spittle gathering on his lips.

Alone for three hundred and twenty days and nights. Kek-kek-kek. Grievous sin. Debts must be paid.

He continues reciting, his voice shaking: "And the Word was God...In him was life–"

I slam his Bible closed. "There are no demons within me." I stretch out my hand and hold my palm over a candle. "The debts are paid," I say softly. "She paid them."

The monk stares, his face terrified and confused. He slaps my hand away from the flame. "You are mad," he croaks.

Quork-quork-quork, kek-kek-kek.

I sit back on my bench and rub a thumb over my reddened palm.

He slowly crosses himself, forehead to heart, left shoulder to right, then takes a deep hiccupping breath. "I have made inquiries," he says cautiously, "and no one saw you for nearly a fortnight after the Feast of the Epiphany." Suspicion curls his upper lip. "The same time Roberval was killed."

I smile at the irony he does not see. "The Epiphany is a time for revelation, *Père*, not concealment." I clasp my hands to cover my palm. "No one in Nontron ever sees me. Not really."

"Do not speak to me in riddles." He pulls at his beard. "I have learned that for nearly a fortnight you were not here to teach the girls."

"I was ill. Confined to my garret."

"Ill?" he says. "With what?"

"Pox."

"Your face bears no scars." The Franciscan takes another stuttering breath to tamp down his fear. "You survived for twenty-seven months on the Isle of Demons, nearly a year alone." His mouth pulls to one side. "Traveling to Paris? Killing your uncle? That would have been as nothing to you."

"*Au contraire, Père*, it would have been something...a great pleasure. Had I done it."

The air is warm and wet, and I have left the window open. Earlier I placed a bit of raw fish on the sill – the tail and some skin cleaned of scales. Foolish to share my food with the cat. Yet I hope she will come.

I consider my palm and wonder if I should prick the blister.

I do not remember illness. Nor do I remember the Feast of the Epiphany or traveling rutted snowy roads or the crowded streets of Paris. Scores of times in my dreams I have hid in the shadows, then leapt out and slit his throat. But if I had awaken and felt his sticky blood on my hands, would I not recall that particular satisfaction?

A deep chuckling: *an instrument of justice...or of murder?*

"Justice, not murder. But it was not I."

La vengeance. Debts must be paid.

"*Oui*, but it was not I who extracted payment."

La vengeance. La justice. Le meurtre.

"There are many who wished him dead." I think

of the pockmarked man. "Perhaps one of Roberval's own colonists was the murderer."

Did he visit me? Or was that only a dream? I see the glint of gold and silver, hear the clink-clink-clink of coins.

La vengeance. La meurtrière. Murderer. La culpabilité.

Did I give him money to kill Roberval?

Perhaps. But I know that the voices cannot always be trusted. It was they who woke me from death with their whispers and their laughter, they who called me to life so they could taunt and harass – and make me remember: *N'oubliez pas.* When I stood and walked away from the crypt, they followed after me: swirls of sapphire, ruby, emerald, and onyx. Carrying the sweet scent of spices, they wrapped themselves about my shoulders, tangled themselves in my hair, and clung to my ears. *N'oubliez pas. Do not forget. Saved by our grace, not God's. Her sin, not yours.*

I did not fear them. What could they do? I was not afraid of dying. I was not afraid of God, and so I feared nothing.

Sometimes, on frigid moonless nights, I could see the voices in the sky: azure, jade, and amber, shimmering veiled dancers on an ebony stage sprinkled with diamonds. I could hear their rustling whispers: teasing, accusing, comforting, duplicitous. I would shout to the black sky, answering their taunts and rebukes.

When I walked away from Marguerite and her

sin, I had no fear of the sea's ravenous white-toothed maw or the fierce red-clawed winds. Let them rage against me. I did not care.

At night, from the entrance of the cave, I saw wolves' copper eyes and heard their susurrant movements through intertwined branches. Their howls and yips pierced the black crepe of night like silver needles, but I was not afraid. I went out and walked among them. They recognized a kindred savagery in my eyes and kept a wary distance.

I was not afraid of the ravens. Marguerite had shunned them. Birds of death, she had called them, omens of evil. I welcomed them and acknowledged them as confederates. Like me, they feared nothing and mocked everything. I learned their irreverent language of croaks, murmurs, and chuckles: *quork-quork-quork, pruk-pruk-pruk, kmm-mm-mm, cark-cark-cark, kek-kek-kek.* In a voice as raspy as theirs, I answered.

Even now – should I wish to do so – I could tell Marguerite's story more easily and truthfully in the language of ravens than in the tangled and treacherous words of men.

I hear a soft thud. The cat has jumped up on the windowsill. Trying to subdue the wildness in my eyes, I will her to stay. She surveys the room: the small table, the hearth, the black pot, the narrow bed, then finally, my face. Black slits widen in serpentine eyes. She snatches the bit of fish and leaps away, before I can stand, and long before I can put my fingers into her ragged fur, soft and matted, wet from the rain.

I light a beeswax candle to ward off the dark.

Scrape of stone upon stone. Each morning I added to the lines Marguerite had drawn, but I no longer cared what day it was, and every day, except when the fierce winds and snow forced me to stay within the cave, I walked, following the ravens wherever they led, though I would not go near to the cliff from which Damienne had fallen.

In the company of ravens, I walked the island: end to end, perimeter, heights and depths, sometimes trudging over windswept rock, sometimes through pockets of deep snow. I counted the strides: one hundred and fifty-six from the cave to the nearest fresh water, eight hundred and four from the cave to the inlet where Michel had built the canvas shelters, nine hundred and fourteen from the cave to the harbour, nine hundred and eighty-two from the summit to the sea.

When the sea froze, I walked across hills and valleys of rafted ice, the sharp edges slicing into the soles of Michel's boots. Four hundred and twelve strides from my island to the next.

I found nothing but more rocks and trees, snow and ice.

All the while I walked, the ravens played in the snow, bathing, diving into it, tossing beakfuls onto glossy black feathers and then shaking it off again. They mocked the snow and ice and the sleet-filled wind. They mocked hunger. They would snap their bills, fly high into the air and spiral down, sometimes alone, sometimes in pairs, spiralling around each other. Always they chattered, to each other and to me: *quork-quork-quork, pruk-pruk-pruk, kek-kek-kek*. I learned their names: Kyree, Prikoo, Karkae, Quakaa, Konkaree. I could not discern who was female and who was male, and they would not say. Curiously, that pleased me.

On clear days the sun warmed the flat stone beside the entrance of the cave. From that broad red rock, Marguerite had kept watch on the harbour, waiting for a ship with white sails. I kept watch, but I waited for nothing.

I would sit beneath the sun's unblinking eye and consider the changing blues and greens of the ice and the sea. I studied the ochre, grey, and pink of the solid rock lining the harbour and of the high stone cliffs beside me, patterned like an artist's oils with curious patches of mottled black and bright green. I listened to the melody of the ice hissing and cracking and booming.

I was queen of all I surveyed: Queen of the Isle of Demons, my only subjects the chittering sparrows and screeching gulls, the silent rabbits and mice. The ravens and the voices would never bend to my will. They were my companions, not my subjects, and they set up a constant babble, intermingling, interrupting, so that I sometimes longed for the silence Marguerite had known.

I did not fear, but neither did I welcome, Damienne's visits. She came to me often, nearly every night for several weeks. Still gaunt, face skeletal, she came and sat too near to the fire, as if in death she could not warm herself. She moved her mouth in a mumble, as if she too were listening to the voices, and arguing. Her eyes accused when she showed me the bloody wounds on her calves.

Be gone from here, I said. I am not her.

Sin, Marguerite, grievous sin, she hissed.

Again and again I repeated the same words: Marguerite meant only to feed Michella, whom you loved, and she paid for what she did. I am not her.

Sin, Marguerite, grievous sin.

Her sin, not mine.

You did not bury my bones. Naked, they click and rattle in the wind. You let the ravens dance upon them. Damienne shivered then and put her hands into the fire, but her flesh did not burn.

The voices on my shoulders whispered: *Leapt. Le suicide. Impardonnable.*

What about your sin, Damienne? I said, the voices giving me courage. You didn't fall. You leapt.

They pushed me.

Who?

The demons.

There are no demons.

Sin, Marguerite, grievous sin.

She is dead. I am not her.

I hear the voices now: *Grievous sin. La perversité. Impardonnable. Debts must be paid.*

"Her sin, not mine," I answer. "I am not her."

I light another candle and search for a bit of cheese to place on the windowsill, but can find nothing. Nothing but the ebony feather. I cradle it in my hands and remember. That memory is mine, not Marguerite's, and it is the only one I choose.

I was not afraid of dying, and yet I fought to live. The powder had become useless, so I no longer bothered to carry the heavy musket with me. I could not shoot the few deer I saw, but managed to net some partridge and gulls and to snare a rabbit now and again. I chopped holes in the ice of the ponds and caught fish. Sometimes I was so hungry I ate the fish raw: scales, bones, entrails, everything. I boiled old bones again and again until the water stayed clear, and then I boiled pieces of hide and seaweed. I stripped the inner bark from trees, the buds from their branches, pulled up dead brown grasses to simmer into a broth. I dug through snow to find the few berries I'd missed the previous fall. I dug for roots, using the axe and the dagger, but the earth was frozen and unforgiving.

I sucked on hardened globs of resin I pried from the bark of trees. I even sucked on small stones and shells just to have something in my mouth. But I did not return to the carcass that was not Damienne.

I began to see that everything was true. And not true. All of it mattered. None of it mattered. The ravens, my hunger, the wind and the sea, the snow, the dreams and the apparitions, the rocks and the trees. The voices. All of it was my life. All of it was my death. No angels. No demons. Only the spirits of that place, *les esprits de cet endroit*. Neither good nor evil.

The ravens led me to carrion: a seal carcass, its rotting halted by snow and ice; bones of deer, not yet picked clean; fish heads; the scattered shells of mussels, whelks, and crabs. Heads tilted, the ravens studied me with discerning black eyes, then flashed white eyelids and allowed me eat beside them, picking and grubbing, murmuring and mumbling. *Km-mm-mm. Kek-kek-kek.*

I followed them everywhere, except to the place where the bones that were not Damienne lay.

One morning, after a full moon, several weeks after Michella's death, or perhaps a month, maybe two – I cannot recall and it does not matter – the ravens led me to the rock summit behind the cave. A crevice about three paces in length and breadth had been swept clean of snow and ice. A large packet, wrapped in hide and covered by a thin layer of new snow, lay within the crevice.

I thought at first the packet was of my own imagining. I glanced back at the ravens. They flashed white eyelids and shifted quietly on bare rock, spreading and shaking black feathers then settling them again. *Km-mm-mm.*

I knelt down and brushed away the snow. On top of the packet lay a small pouch of rose silk tied with a fine thread. I sat back on my heels, stunned: rose silk from Marguerite's dress. Somewhere on the island was a man, or a woman! An Indian...or *un esprit*. I scanned the fresh snow, but there were no tracks but my own and the ravens'.

Fingers fumbling, I untied the thread binding the silk and smoothed the wrinkled cloth. In the centre of the silk square lay dried shavings that smelled of bark and leaves and earth. Tea? Medicine? Poison?

I set the shavings aside and reached for Michel's dagger, then stopped, deciding instead to untie the larger bindings carefully. I unfolded the dark hide, the inner side a lustrous white fur. A thick plait of sweet-smelling grass lay atop sheets of thin bark. I lifted the bark sheets and saw strips of dried meat, smoked fish, and a small basket filled with a mixture of fat and dried berries. The stitching on the bark basket was evenly spaced, meticulous. A flowing pattern of flowers, leaves, and vines had been etched along the edge. Who had taken such care with this basket? Who had left this gift?

Un cadeau, un cadeau. Km-mm-mm.

I did not know if the words came from the voices or the ravens, did not know if I was dreaming. I did not care. I tore chunks from the greasy smoked fish and stuffed them into my mouth. Even before I could swallow the fish, I bit into the tough meat, ripped off a thin strip, then chewed and chewed, spit dripping down my chin, my teeth and jaws aching with the effort. I dipped my fingers into the berries and fat and scooped the mixture into my mouth. I could not stop myself from eating. I did not care that the food might be poisoned.

The ravens began shifting on their stony perches, claws scraping. One called out in loud *quorks*, another in softer *pruk-pruk-pruks*. I understood, and put out bits of smoked fish. Kyree flew down, circled the fish in a stately strut, like a gentleman or lady at court, then picked up a small piece. As if waiting for this signal, the other ravens descended and snatched the bits of fish from the snow, leaving only their tracks and the imprints of their wings.

I folded what was left of the food back into the hide, tied it loosely with the sinew, and followed the ravens back to my cave. That night I slept beneath the warm white fur, the silk bundle clutched in my hand. I dreamed of fluttering ebony feathers, and Damienne did not visit.

I look away from the candle and see iridescent green eyes. We stare at each other, the cat and I. She places her front feet on the windowsill and sniffs the air, all the while watching me. She sits back, licks a front paw and passes it over her face and whiskers.

I take one step forward, and she is gone.

Isabelle tugs on her father's hand as she closes the door behind her. Head tilted proudly, she glances toward the other girls. "Madame de Roberval, Papa would speak with you about my Latin."

Lafrenière appraises me and the classroom, but dark curls, much like Isabelle's own, soften his stern face. "Madame de Roberval," he says formally. He places a hand to his black doublet and dips his head. His white linen cuff is frayed. "Monsieur Lafrenière," he says.

I have already met Isabelle's father, and I know that his family, though noble, is as poor as Marguerite's and Michel's. From Isabelle, I know this as well: Lafrenière is a man who has read about Jean-François de la Roque, Sieur de Roberval, as well as the king's cosmographer, André Thevet.

"Isabelle's study of Latin displeases you?" I say bluntly.

"*Au contraire*," he says. "I approve of my daughter studying Latin. Isabelle is to learn whatever is within her capabilities. And I believe her capabilities to be quite large."

Puffed with importance, Isabelle stands tall beside her father.

"I will not have her hobbled by...by a *limited* education." He pauses to be certain I have understood.

I have. My harsh sentiments toward him soften, but only slightly. Lafrenière is like Marguerite's father. He goes without so that he can buy his daughter books, paper, ink, and candles. He shares with her his words and ideas. Isabelle often chatters about geography, alchemy, and God: conversations she has had with her father. I am leery, though, that Lafrenière has come to ask me to teach her to pray in Latin.

"If Isabelle is to learn Latin," he continues, "then she must learn more than a list of words. I insist that she study conjugations, declensions, and syntax. May I see the Latin grammar you are using?"

"Of course." I wave a hand toward the book.

He picks up the small grammar and caresses the

tooled images on the leather cover. His expression softens and he looks as if he might bestow kisses upon the book. His hands, the fingernails clean and square, turn the vellum pages slowly, careful not to tear or crease them. "*Bien, bien,*" he murmurs, then "*bona*" in Latin. At long last, he lays the book aside and turns to me, as if his thoughts are now on Marguerite.

I wonder then if his expressed concerns about Latin are merely a ruse so that he can come to the school and examine more closely the creature who has lived on the Isle of Demons. Would Lafrenière use Isabelle to satisfy his own prurient interests? Perhaps he has instructed her to ask me questions about the island.

I do not try to tame the savagery lurking in my eyes.

He smoothes his neatly trimmed beard, all self-assurance gone. He takes a step closer. Too close. He smells of russet oak leaves and earth. "Madame de Roberval," he says softly, "my brother knew Monsieur de Roberval…" His voice trails off.

"Half-brother," Isabelle corrects. "My half-uncle."

I step away from him. Lafrenière's whispered confidences are of no interest to me. Most of the nobles knew Roberval. He charmed, and used, many.

Lafrenière looks at Isabelle then back at me. My disinterest surprises him, and he does not know how to proceed. I will not help him. I will answer no more questions about Roberval, Marguerite, or me.

He clears his throat. "I must go now," he says to

Isabelle. He straightens his shoulders and tugs at the hem of his doublet. "Learn your lessons well." He nods curtly, then leaves.

"Embroidery," I say. "You will *all* work on embroidery this morning."

"Madame de Roberval," says Isabelle, "might I study Latin? Please?"

"*Non.*" I take some satisfaction in her disappointed face.

She picks up my hand. Her small finger pokes at the blister. "What happened?" she asks maliciously. Then, without waiting for an answer, she drops my hand and flounces off to get her needles, thread, and hoops.

I curl my fingers over the blistered palm. I feel no pain now. I felt no pain then. Only dreadful cold.

I could not waste fat on my hands. They cracked and bled, but I felt nothing but the cold. The whole of my life was finding food and scratching a line on the wall for each passing day. The whole of my life was the ravens and the voices. I did not long for Michel or Michella. I did not long for rescue. I no longer cared about Roberval and his ships.

I longed only for food and warmth – and to meet who, or what, had left the packet of food and the silk bundle.

Isabelle's fingertips are already dimpled and red with needle pricks. Her stitches are long and uneven, and the linen square is soiled with sweat from her hands.

I relent, as bored as she is with the tedium of

embroidery. "You may study Latin now," I say.

She grins at me and rushes to the grammar. She stops short, rubs her sweaty palms on her skirt, and resists touching the book. Bouncing up and down on her toes, she waits until I open it for her.

"Vocabulary for a while yet," I say, "then perhaps, conjugation."

Isabelle peers at the page. "*Juth, jurith,*" she tries to pronounce through her half-teeth.

"*Jus, juris,*" I repeat.

"*Lexth, legith,*" she lisps.

"*Lex, legis.*"

"Caesar! *Expedition!*" she exclaims, pleased to have recognized a word. "Just like *l'expédition.*"

"*Expeditio,*" I correct. "The Latin is *expeditio.*"

"Was it very, very awful?" she asks cautiously.

Face rigid, I point at the Latin grammar. I will not listen to the questions her imperious father has instructed her to ask, and most certainly I will not answer.

Obediently she studies the page. After a few moments she whispers, "What was it like…being all alone? I would have been afraid."

"Latin, Isabelle. You are studying Latin."

She looks at me, her eyes coy. "What is the Latin word for Indians?"

"I do not know." My words are cold and clipped. "Perhaps it would be *barbarus.*"

"*Barbaruth,*" she says softly, then bows her head and studies the words.

The morning after the next full moon the ravens led me to the second packet of food, in the same rock crevice. Again a rose silk bundle filled with dark shavings lay on top. I looked for tracks, but again could find none but my own and the ravens'.

Who had left the packets? Was a spirit laying bait the way I laid bait for gulls?

No matter. I was far too hungry and cold to turn away from the food and the warm furs.

I began to feel as if I were being watched. Someone – or something – knew I was there. It did not surprise me that the feeling was more comfort than threat.

Near the time of the next full moon the ravens persuaded me to conceal myself near the rock crevice. Wrapped in the warm furs that had been left with the packets, I kept watch for several days and nights, the ravens with me. Still, we nearly missed him.

He came at dusk, emerging silently from the fog. A tall figure clothed in thick dark hides, he carried a packet similar to the other two. I looked about, wondering if others like him would spring out of the fog and kill me or take me captive, but there seemed to be no one else. Only him.

Kneeling on one knee, he cleared snow from the crevice and laid down the packet. When he pulled back his hood, I saw that his face was smooth and bronzed, neither frightful nor handsome. A black feather fastened atop his dark hair fluttered in the light wind, a rasping accompaniment to his murmured words. He spoke softly, his face tilted upward. Then he sang, the quavering melody like nothing I'd ever heard. The ravens listened, heads cocked, but feathers sleek and relaxed, as if they recognized his voice and his song. As if they knew him.

Small fingers touch my palm. Isabelle gasps. "Madame de Roberval, what happened?" This time her face is concerned.

"*Nihilum.*"

"Nothing?" she says.

I turn the page. "Continue your lessons."

She looks at the blister, then back at the grammar. "*Nihilum,*" she says uncertainly. "*Silentium, solitudo.*"

I studied the kneeling figure, his head now bowed. An Indian? A spirit?

Who, or what, did he believe I was? A demon? One he could appease with gifts? Or did he believe me to be simply a woman in need?

My unfeeling numbness collapsed. I felt an unbearable ache. I wanted him to come to me – to love me or to kill me – but not to leave me alone. Not alone.

I stepped forward. Stay here! I begged. Please. Stay here.

His head jerked up. Startled, but neither afraid nor unafraid. Still kneeling, he watched me, as if waiting for me to speak again.

I took another step forward. Stay here, I asked again and reached out a hand. I wanted to touch him, to know that he was a man.

He placed before him the dried shavings he held in his hand. He stood, murmured a few words, and then slowly backed away from me, nodding and continuing to speak words I could not understand. I tried to follow, but he disappeared into the fog like an apparition.

It was dark, the moon covered by fog, and I could not see to follow his trail. By morning his trail, if there had ever been one, was covered with new snow, and I wondered if I had only conjured or dreamed his coming. Even so, I felt bereft.

"*Desolatio*," Isabelle lisps.

"*Desolatio*," I repeat, but I think of the packet of food, topped with the bundle of rose silk. And I remember the ebony feather.

"The Devil is quite active among the natives there." The Franciscan leans toward me. "It would be understandable if demons troubled you while you were alone." His smile is conspiratorial and expectant, as if his wheedling will prompt me to share secrets.

"Indeed, the Devil has so bewitched the natives they believe that those who die disappear like smoke," he whispers, "and the soul is changed into wind or a raven or a bear."

For my days are vanished like smoke…I am like a night raven in the house. Km-mm-mm.

"Did you see Indians while you were on the island?"

"*Non*, she did not."

"No tracks, no signs? Nothing to indicate that anyone lived or traveled near the island?"

"*Nihilum*."

"*Nihilum?*"

"Latin, *Père*. It means nothing."

Thevet smoothes his cassock over his belly, then picks up a quill. I hear the rasp and remember another feather, a black feather with a purple sheen that turned in the wind.

I could think of nothing but him, not my hunger nor the cold. I ceased to care whether he was man or spirit. Every evening, holding the dark shavings in my hand just as he had held them, I waited near the crevice. I breathed in the heavy aromatic scent and hoped desperately he would come. Every morning I checked for packets, then went in search of tracks. The ravens came with me, but either could not, or would not, lead me to him.

Every night, awake or asleep, I dreamed of him.

The voices taunted: *Le sauvage ou l'esprit. Le comportement scandaleux.* And encouraged: *L'amour et le désir. Le compagnon.*

I dreamed of him coming to me and touching me as Michel had touched Marguerite. I could feel his lips on mine, his warm breath on my neck. I could see my face reflected in his mahogany eyes. My hands on my breasts and thighs became his hands, and my fingers explored his body beneath the deer hides. I woke to the scent of his skin, like the moss from which he had sprung.

When I found him again we would live on the island, just he and I. We would use only the language of touch and the calls of ravens. We would have no need for words, but I would learn his prayers and I would pray to the spirits of that place.

Thevet taps the nib of his quill against the paper, a steady tap-tap-tap. I look up and see a white weasel sitting on his shoulder, flicking its black-tipped tail, its pointed teeth bared at the monk's impatience. "So strange that there were no Indians on the island," he says. "Not even in spring, when the seals are there?"

"*Non.*"

"They are quite proficient in using seals." He proceeds to explain once again how Indians use seals for food and clothes. "The Indians are quite clever, Marguerite…"

I pretend to listen.

I awoke one night to the sound of someone calling my name. Struggling up from sleep, I looked around in the dim light given off by the banked coals.

Michel, strong and robust, cheeks rosy, smile dazzling. He leaned forward to stroke my face. Marguerite, he said softly. *Je t'aime.* I love you.

I flinched away from his touch. *Non*, I said, I am not her.

His smile disappeared. *La putain,* he said. You have been unfaithful to me.

Marguerite loved you. I do not. Return from whence you came.

His lips parted to reveal a skull's malevolent grin.

I come from nowhere, he said, and you will follow, faithless whore.

You were unfaithful to her, I countered. And unfaithful to Michella. You would not fight to live.

Michella? I know nothing of any Michella.

I slapped at his face. It was like slapping at fog. And then, like a flame snuffed, he was gone.

"The oil, reddish in colour, they drink with their meals…"

Just before the next full moon, I wrapped within a scrap of rose silk a pearl ring Marguerite had kept in the trunk. I tied the silk with sinew and placed it in the crevice where he had left the packets. I hoped the ring would show him, man or spirit, that I was only a woman.

I worried. Would he come? Or had I scared him away? When the seals arrived and then the ducks and seabirds, would he continue to bring food?

Did he believe that I hungered only for food?

I waited. Finally he came, emerging once again from the fog. I wanted to rush forward, but I held myself back. He laid down the packet and picked up the silk pouch. He was unhurried as he unwrapped the ring. He placed it in his palm, the pearl like a pale full moon. The feather in his hair danced in the soft wind.

I stepped forward then, my words soft but insistent, my hands clasped as if in prayer. Please, please, I begged, take me with you…or come, be with me. Do not leave me alone.

"Those natives who dwell inland towards

Baccaleos are wicked and cruel." The words slip into my ears as Thevet continues to lecture. "They mask their faces, not with masks or cloths, but by painting them with diverse colours, especially blue and red, so to render themselves hideous."

The ravens mumbled and murmured: *km-mm-mm, km-mm-mm.* I opened my hand to show him the bits of dried bark cradled in my palm. His dark eyes, as discerning as the ravens', considered me, and I slowly extended two fingers to touch his black hair, as smooth as the rose silk. His cheek was solid and warm, and I saw a small white scar above his eyebrow. A man, not a spirit.

Ever so slowly, as if he were trying to capture a butterfly, he reached out and touched my lips, brushing a thumb across them, his warm fingers cupping my chin.

Lost in the pleasure and comfort of touch, I closed my eyes. Then I heard the ravens call out: *quork-quork-quork, kek-kek-kek.*

My eyes flew open. He was gone, vanished into the fog. The pearl ring and an ebony feather lay atop the square of rose silk.

"These men are big and strong and go around clothed in skins." Thevet gives a small disdainful laugh. "They draw up their hair in a top-knot just like we bind up horses' tails over here."

"The feather."

He nods. "*Oui*, they decorate themselves with feathers."

I lift my palm to my nose and smell the heavy

aroma of dried bark and leaves.

The Franciscan thrusts out his fat lower lip, his face perplexed. "How did you manage to survive that winter?"

"Ravens."

"You ate ravens?"

"*Non*, *Père*, I followed them to food."

"I!" he exclaims. "Finally you have said *I*." He takes a deep satisfied breath as if he has just completed an arduous task. "At last…at long last, I have made you accept that you are Marguerite."

He does not understand. He will never understand.

"Following the ravens? Clever, but was the food not already dead and rotting?" His face wears his revulsion. "Why did you not shoot something? A deer or a bear?"

"The powder lost its force."

"How did you protect yourself?"

I shrug. "There was no need."

"But you could not have lived on *carrion*."

"I snared rabbits, ate tree bark and roots, seaweed."

"You could not have survived an entire winter on that, Marguerite. You must have been helped…by something."

I hear their voices: *Saved by our grace, not God's. Marguerite is dead, but you must live. Her sin, not yours.*

"God," I say flatly.

"God?"

I try to bolster my lies with enthusiasm. "When demons came to tempt me, screeching and howling, it was God who helped me, God who provided a shield against wolves and bears." I wave my hands, palms out, my angry wound visible. I try to make my voice high and light, filled with awe. "It was as if his angels filled my belly. I did not hunger. When the angels appeared, the demons fled."

The Franciscan's face is suffused with wonder. He bends over his paper and scribbles frenetically, recording my lies. "What did the angels look like?" he asks, not looking up.

"They wore shining white robes. They had golden wings and golden hair."

"How many?"

"Three." Always there must be three – or seven.

"How big?"

"As big as a tall man, but slender." I look behind the Franciscan and see a smooth bronzed face, a small white scar above the eyebrow, an ebony feather turning in the wind.

Thevet strokes his gold cross. "How did you know the angels were not demons disguised as angels?"

Kek-kek-kek. How long, O Lord? How long? Cark-cark-cark.

I pause to listen, and to think. I hear the scrape of stone upon stone: three hundred and twenty days, three hundred and twenty nights. Alone. But not alone.

"I tested them," I say finally. "When I began reciting psalms the angels stayed. When I prayed they bowed their heads."

Thevet closes his eyes and bows his own head. "The perfect test, Marguerite. The perfect test." He looks up. "And did you express to them your contrition for your grievous sins?"

I stare at his sanctimonious face.

Grievous sin. Impardonnable. La pénitence. Her sin, not yours.

"*Oui*," I say. "The angels offered absolution."

Quork-quork-quork. Kek-kek-kek.

He dips his quill in black ink to record what I have said. He seems to have forgotten that only yesterday he believed me possessed. Now he believes I've seen and talked with angels.

L' idiot, l'imbécile.

"*Oui*," I answer.

As he writes, the monk runs his tongue over his fat lips, as if he finds my description of angels provocative.

The voices laugh: *Le Père pervers. Le Père lascif.*

"And in the spring," I say, "the angels brought the seals...just like manna from heaven."

Le cadeau. Le cadeau. Les esprits de cet endroit.

I see Marguerite, heavy with Michella, sabre raised. Like her, I filled my belly with their rich flesh and their fat, but unlike Marguerite, I did not believe the seals to be a gift from Michel or from God. The seals were a gift from the spirits of that place. They were a gift to the bears and to the ravens. The seals were their own gift to themselves.

The ravens surrounded me and ate their fill. We feasted alongside great white bears and their cubs. I did not fear them or their *huff-huff-huff* or their enormous paws. They looked at me, their small black eyes mildly curious, and accepted my presence among them. Then they killed seals as they had always killed seals, until all that was white – snow and ice and bear and seal – was crimson.

"Then the water opened close to shore, and the ducks and geese came. The seabirds nested. The demons – and the angels – left me alone then."

Solitaire, solitaire.

"*Non*, not alone," I murmur, but the Franciscan does not hear me.

I would sit within the cave and stroke the ebony feather, listening to its rasp. I would call him to me. And he would come. Silently, out of the grey smoke, he would come and slip beneath the furs to lie beside me on the pink rock.

L'esprit. L'amour. Le compagnon.

I feel again the touch of his lips, the rough skin of his fingertips, the silkiness of his hair on my face. I feel the smooth muscles of his arms and legs, the strength of his back, the filling of the hollowness within.

I smell the scent of his skin, like clean dry moss.

He never said a word, nor did he smile. I was careful, very careful, because sometimes I would reach out for him and my hands would grasp only furs or my fingers would slip through his chest and he would vanish into the smoke of the fire. I tried not to fall asleep, because when I awoke he would be gone and I would be alone. Always.

Solitaire, solitaire.

"*Oui,*" I say. "Alone. Always."

"But God was with you, Marguerite. God was always with you."

I wake in the garret, the feel of rough granite beneath my fingertips. The cave? Or the Church of the Innocents? But I smell moss, not blood. I reach for the ebony feather, hoping to call him to me, but he is distant now. Too far away to call back. He cannot come to me in this place.

I stand and light a candle, then see luminous green eyes at the open window. I creep toward the cat. Wary, she remains still, tail swishing from side to side. Her swollen belly stands out from her thin body. Very, very slowly I reach out. When my fingers are only inches from her yellow head she flees, bouncing away on her stiff hind leg.

I search until I find a bit of cheese to leave on the windowsill.

It is the sabbath. I am free of the girls and I am free of Thevet. I walk the muddy paths through the woods and fields outside Nontron, hoping to hear the soft beat of ebony wings. I discovered when I returned to France that ravens speak the same language here as there, and crows speak a similar dialect. It is like comparing the *patois* of Angoulême to that of Périgueux.

The crows are nearly as clever as the ravens. They follow the farmers when they sow barley and rye. The farmers turn on them and flap their arms as if they too would fly away, but as soon as the men turn their backs the crows return. Then the farmers make their children stand in the fields to shoo away the birds.

The crows return now, on the sabbath, when the farmers and their children are in church, or indoors. The morning sun gives their black feathers an emerald sheen. The birds eat greedily, and I am tempted to join them, to pick up the grain and grind it into flour. On the island I had no bread, and now I cannot get enough.

I step into the dark comfort of the woods and am surrounded by tall maples and beeches, branches newly leaved. I breathe in the fragrance of green. Studying a new maple leaf, I trace the intricate lines within, stroke its softness, and put it to my cheek.

Ravens gather in the trees above, *quorking* and *pruking* their greetings. I hear their wings, like welcoming whispers, rustling, sliding, rasping. Their claws scrape lightly as they grip the bark. One shuffles along a branch, then wipes her thick bill near her feet. They ruffle their feathers, then settle them again, knowing that I mean them no harm, that I have come only to rest in their company. I listen to their soft conversation, *km-mm-mm*, and know they will ask me no questions.

I am startled then to see Monsieur Lafrenière on the path. His lanky frame strides toward me. When he raises an arm and waves, the ravens rise silently into the crystalline sky and are gone. I turn and hurry away, pretending I have not seen him. I do not look back or slow my pace until I have climbed the stairs to my garret.

Gasping for breath, I fling open the door. The yellow-striped cat is curled on the bed. She jumps down. Body held low, her belly nearly dragging the floor, she slinks out through the window.

I close the window. I will not think of Lafrenière. Instead I study the small circles of glass, tinted blue-green, as if the glass contains the sea. And then I think of the cat. She was sleeping on my bed. Her eyes held wariness, but she was *on my bed*. I open the window, hoping she will return.

There is a loud banging at the door. "Madame de Roberval," he calls out in a loud whisper. "Please, I must speak with you."

I say nothing. What can this man want from me?

"I know you are in there. Please, come to the door." His voice is urgent.

"*Non*, I will not," I say through the door.

They taunt me then: *Propriety. Une femme solitaire. Un homme. Cark-cark-cark. Scandalous.*

They know I care nothing for propriety. But neither does Lafrenière – or he would not come to my garret, alone, to see me. Yet I am grateful to the voices: they have given me reason to send him away.

"I am alone," I say. "You must go away." I put

my ear to the door to listen for footsteps descending the stairs. I hear only the shout of a child from the street below and the distant voice of a robin, its thin warble repeated again and again.

Finally he answers, "That is not why I have come, Madame de Roberval. If you wish we can walk abroad where everyone can see us. But I will not leave until I have spoken to you."

"We can speak of Isabelle's Latin tomorrow."

"I do not wish to speak of Isabelle. Or Latin. I wish to speak of…other things."

"What other things?" But I already know. Lafrenière would ask me about Marguerite.

"Please. Open the door."

"I will answer none of your questions."

"Then I will ask no questions. But I will not leave until you open the door."

I crack it open.

His face is flushed, his forehead beaded with sweat. He smells of mud and fresh air, and stale wool. "Please," he says. "May I come in? I cannot speak to you through the door."

I stand for a long time, staring through the narrow gap.

"Shall we walk then?"

I open the door wider and Lafrenière steps in. His breeches and doublet are rumpled. Brown mud clings to his stockings and boots. His white collar and cuffs are smudged and threadbare. He looks around, then remains standing. There is only the bench near the hearth and the bed.

I close the door behind him. He removes his cap and holds it before him, as if expecting me to invite him to speak. I cross my arms over my chest. Let him say whatever he has to say and then leave, quickly.

He proceeds without my invitation. "My half-brother knew Monsieur de Roberval."

"So you have told me."

"I want you to know," he blurts, "that I believe it was Roberval who was the sinner."

I shrug. I do not care what Lafrenière believes about Roberval.

"My brother, my half-brother, went with him on his expedition. He did not return."

Michel? I put a hand to my heart to quiet its loud beating.

"Saintonge…Roberval's pilot. He told me my brother drowned when he went with Roberval on one of his forays from Charlesbourg Royal."

Non, not Michel. My heart slows.

"Searching for gold and jewels," Lafrenière says bitterly. "My brother drowned for Roberval's folly and greed."

I realize then that Lafrenière's brother was among the pathetic noblemen who stood aside, hands folded over their codpieces, and did nothing when Roberval abandoned Marguerite, Michel, and Damienne to their deaths.

I cannot hold back my snort of contempt. "So you wish me to weep for him?"

"*Non*, of course not, but I thought…"

"What?"

"That it might be some comfort…" He searches for words. "I do not believe that you and your husband did anything wrong." He pinches the brim of his cap, folding and unfolding. "Or scandalous…"

So this is what he wants. Monsieur Lafrenière would have me whet his carnal appetites. He thinks that if he offers forgiveness and understanding, I will be eager to speak of such things, then he will smile unctuously and watch my mouth speak of lascivious behaviour, desire, scandal.

"You are mistaken," I say. "That was not me."

He steps back. "Are you not Marguerite de la Roque de Roberval?"

"You said you would ask no questions."

"Was it not you that Roberval left on the Isle of Demons?"

"She died. I lived."

"I don't understand."

"We have talked too long," I say. "You must leave now."

"*Non*, please. Not before I beg your forgiveness on behalf of my brother. He was young and he lacked the courage to oppose the viceroy."

I see again the eyes averted, hands folded over codpieces, balance shifting from foot to foot. "Many lacked such courage," I say.

"Please, I beg your forgiveness."

"Forgiveness is not mine to give."

"But you–"

"It was not me!"

Lafrenière cocks his head, just like the Franciscan. He stares at me for a long time, eyes the colour of iron, deep lines at the corners. He is not a man without worries – or intelligence. His grey eyes soften then and he nods slowly, as if he understands. "Of course," he whispers.

What can he possibly understand about Marguerite? Or me?

He persists, speaking softly now. "Saintogne's biggest regret, he told me, was that he could not persuade Roberval to return with Cartier to France." He presses the cap to his chest. "And that he could not prevail upon the viceroy to punish y–" He stops, then continues, "to punish Marguerite in a different way."

"I know nothing of Roberval or Saintogne...or Marguerite."

Lafrenière's eyes glisten, as if he might weep. He goes down on one knee. "Please, let me beg your forgiveness on behalf of my brother."

"I told you, forgiveness is not mine to give." I turn away from his show of weakness. Just like his half-brother. Weak and lacking courage, fondling his cap instead of his codpiece.

He speaks to my back, his words rushing out, "Roberval should never have taken you...I mean Marguerite...with him. Why take a young noblewoman on an expedition like that?"

Pourquoi? Km-mm-mm. Pourquoi?

"You would have been justified in killing him."

La vengeance. La justice. Murderer.

"Murderer," I answer, turning around.

His flushed cheeks pale. "*Oui*," he says finally. "Roberval was a murderer. And I, for one, am glad he was assassinated." Peering at me warily, he stands.

La culpabilité. Debts must be paid.

"You have said what you came to say. Now you must go."

"Of course." Lafrenière bows his head, a supplicant. "But please think upon what I have told you. And search within your heart for mercy and forgiveness."

I hear mocking laughter: *La pitié et le pardon. Le cœur tendre. Être indulgent, c'est mourir.*

"*Oui*," I agree, "to be soft is to die."

He shakes his head. "*Non*, Madame de Roberval, to be soft is to be merciful." He places a hand on the open door, pauses. "You are bitter...understandably so. But beneath your bitterness lies goodness, and mercy."

Chuckling echoes off the walls: *La bienveillance et la pitié de Marguerite. La bienveillance et la pitié de Marguerite.*

"Please forgive my forwardness, but I can see that in you. And I believe Isabelle sees it as well."

I want to laugh out loud with the voices. No matter what he and Isabelle might wish to see, there is only savagery in me. No goodness, no mercy.

"May I visit you again?" he asks stupidly. "To hear your answer. Perhaps in a more appropriate place...where we can speak of more pleasant things."

"You must go now."

"Of course," he says. "Of course."

He presses his cap between his palms, trying to gather his dignity. Finally Lafrenière dons his cap, squares it, and closes the door behind him.

My day of freedom, my day with the ravens, has been ruined.

I listen to the girls recite prayers to Saint George, slayer of dragons in the defence of young maidens. Tomorrow is the saint's feast day – another day of freedom from the girls and Thevet. The Franciscan will spend the day on bended knee before his Christ, praying for the strength to slay dragons.

For now, though, I must listen to the girls' halting Latin, voices disharmonious, words garbled. Only Isabelle says the words precisely and correctly. I listen for her voice: "O God, who didst grant to Saint George strength and constancy in the various torments which he sustained for our holy faith, we beseech thee to preserve, through his intercession, our faith from wavering and doubt, so that we may serve thee with a sincere heart faithfully unto death."

Isabelle studies me as she recites, as if she would confirm her suspicions that I teach what I do not believe myself. I wonder what her father has told her and what she watches for in my face. Yesterday, after Lafrenière left, I went to the window and examined my reflection in the blue-green glass. I lit a candle and gazed long into the night. I could see no goodness there, no kindness, no mercy. Only the hue and texture of granite.

The striped cat did not come back.

When the girls have finished the prayer and taken up their slates to practise forming letters, Isabelle approaches. She is bored with simple letters and words, but I have no other books to give her.

"Madame de Roberval, Papa has shown me some of his maps. Did you ever see the dragons?"

"I know nothing of dragons."

"You didn't see any?" Her face is bright with the thrill of danger. "Not one? Even way out in the sea?"

"*Nullus,*" I say firmly in Latin.

"Oh." Her shoulders slump in disappointment.

I walk to the window. Isabelle follows relentlessly. Her small hand tugs on my skirt. "But they are very ugly, aren't they?" Her small body shudders. "And dangerous. Do you believe Saint George really killed one? All by himself?"

"Isabelle," I sigh. "I know nothing about dragons."

"But what do you believe?"

"It matters little what I believe. *Nullus.*"

Isabelle considers this a moment, then says, "I saw a very ugly man once. One with scars all over his face. He was like a monster…or a dragon. He came to our door, and Papa let him in." She mimics dragging a leg. "He walked like this."

I spin away to hide my distress. The pockmarked man, Roberval's colonist. He was not a dream, not an apparition.

"They went into Papa's study." Isabelle covers a mischievous smile behind her hand. "I hid behind the door and peeked through the keyhole," she confesses.

I hear again Lafrenière's words: *I am glad Roberval was assassinated.*

Did he pay the pockmarked man? Is this what he came to tell me?

Murderer. Le sang rouge. Grievous sin.

"*Non*," I answer softly. "Not murder...justice."

"*Jus, juris,*" Isabelle says in Latin.

The pockmarked man, a slayer of dragons.

Debts must be paid. Km-mm-mm.

"*Oui*, Isabelle, *oui.*"

The Franciscan has already asked, again and again, what I ate that summer. He is infinitely interested in how I survived. He is obsessed with angels and demons. He has made me repeat my rescue by angels so many times that I see them now, with their golden hair and golden wings, hovering above him. They giggle when their wingtips brush the bald circle at the top of his head. He reaches up to scratch it.

"Did many ships pass by the island?"

"A few."

"How many?"

"I did not count."

"You kept careful count of the days but not of the ships?"

"The days are always there, *Père*, but sometimes my eyes conjured sails from the wings of gulls."

The monk's scowl tells me that my answer does not please him, but I cannot explain to him that I did not keep watch for ships because I neither expected, nor wished, to be taken from the island. Every dawn I scraped a new line on the wall, but I did not light a signal fire near the harbour.

Over that summer I gathered and dried berries, collected eggs. I also dried fish and seal meat. Even so, my stores of food remained small because I spent hours studying the colour and shape of each bloom as it appeared: white blossoms sweetly scenting the air, tiny pink bells trailing close to the ground, dark rosy clusters and bunches of white filling the bogs, bright yellow buttercups and daisies dancing in grassy meadows.

My hipbones were sharp and protruding, my fingers like bony claws. Though I had no mirror, I knew my face looked like a skull, the bronzed skin drawn tight over jawbone and cheek.

Nonetheless I was content to live out my life on the island. I no longer cared how long that life would be. I cared only that he would come to me again.

Le compagnon. L'amour et le désir. Les esprits de cet endroit.

I smile inwardly.

"But the sails of the Breton ship were real," says Thevet. "Those were not gulls' wings."

"*Non*, but they might have been."

His bulbous eyes blink at his confusion.

I do not wish to try to explain that I saw and heard many things, that I neither knew, nor cared, what was there and what was not. All of it was there. All of it was real. All of it was my life: the ivory wings of gulls against pewter skies; the granite scrape of stone upon stone; the soft wailing of a child in a silver wind; the spiders weaving the world together, every day, silk threads stitching rock to sea to sky. I studied the lines and cracks in red and grey rock and saw the streets of Paris, Michel's glinting eyes, Damienne's accusing face. I looked at iron-grey clouds and saw doves flying and packs of wolves howling. Sometimes I could see through my hand, to the white bones beneath, then the flesh would close over, but the metallic scent of blood would linger.

I watched ducks and gulls preen and posture, the females dipping their heads under a wing. I saw in them the ladies at court dressed in sparkling jewels and in silks and satins of pale blue, topaz, and amethyst, strutting grandly, circling coyly, feather fans held to porcelain faces. Waves could become an army of snarling white bears, racing ashore and smashing themselves against unmovable rock. And then disappearing into a red wind. I could smell their hot meaty breath and feel their wet fur. But I could also feel their benevolence and indifference. I could feel how their spirits fit that place and accepted me among them.

Sometimes the wind was green, sometimes crimson or indigo, and when it blew softly I could hear the citre, the notes clear and ringing, weaving themselves within the wind. I could hear Marguerite's weary and frightened voice reciting poems, prayers, and psalms. I could hear Michella howling her hunger, never to be satisfied.

I could gaze endlessly into the violet sheen of the ebony feather and see his brown face, his hair like silk, and mahogany eyes. I could float in the smoke of the fire, breathe in the scent of his skin, and watch myself, with him.

And always, always, there were the voices: keening, accusing, cajoling, comforting. And the ravens: *quork-quork-quork, pruk-pruk-pruk, kek-kek-kek, km-mm-mm.* They mocked God and angels – and the Devil and demons. The ravens were often magnanimous, occasionally cruel, but always amused by the world's dark humour.

The summer came and then left again. Green leaves and moss turned to gold and copper, to red, maroon, orange, and purple. An explosion of colour. The ravens chuckled at the irony that such beauty should be the harbinger of the abominable winds and cold to come.

I planned to die on the flat expanse of rock beside the cave. The ravens would feast on my body. I would become one of them and fly above the island with them.

I would be their eucharist: *this is my body...this is my blood.* I would become a spirit of that place. Like him.

"The loneliness, Marguerite. The unimaginable

loneliness." The monk's face is sad, as if he feels the loneliness himself. "Were you not ecstatic to see a ship enter the harbour? Did you not fall on your knees and thank God that you would be rescued? That you would soon be with people again?"

I hear laughter: *Merci beaucoup, merci beaucoup. Kek-kek-kek.*

"What day did the ship come?"

"The twenty-first day of October in 1544. Eight hundred and thirty-one days after Roberval left them."

"Did you see angels then?"

"No angels."

I stared at the ship and simply waited for the sails to disappear or to resolve into white wings and fly off into white clouds. Instead it came closer, and I watched men lower a small boat over the side, along with several large barrels. The water was blue-green, aquamarine closer to shore. Waves caressed the red rock, and the wind blew gently, interwoven with sparkling bits of sun.

"The harbour is deep there," says Thevet. "The ship anchored there to take on fresh water." The Franciscan wants to be certain I understand that the Breton fishermen did not come for Marguerite. They came for water. "What did the men say to you?"

"I do not know."

"What do you mean, you do not know?"

"I could not understand them, *Père*."

Three men rowed toward shore, fishermen, not soldiers, and they talked and laughed as they pulled on the creaking oars, their voices carrying over the water, intermingling with the calls of gulls and ravens. The men jumped into the shallow water and towed their boat ashore, wood scraping on rock.

The ravens retreated and called from a distance, *kek-kek-kek*, warning me. But I was not afraid. I expected the men, the boat, and the ship to vanish, to disappear into the clouds or the sea, or to change into rocks and trees. I did not bother to hide.

When the men looked up and saw me, they scrambled to grab sabres. They stood together and waved their sabres as if I were a wild beast or a demon. I did not move, and one of them stepped forward and spoke, his words vaguely familiar, though I could make no sense of them. His voice was intertwined with all the others.

Demat. Good day. Kek-kek-kek. Bonjour. Who are you? Le sauvage? La sauvagesse? Pruk-pruk-pruk. Demat. Km-mm-mm.

"They thought you were an Indian," the Franciscan says, amused. "A native of those lands. Dressed in hides, feathers in your tangled hair. Skin brown from the sun."

In the face of my silence, the man retreated. The three huddled together again, murmuring to each other, hands gesturing. Their voices became louder, arguing. Still, I could not understand their harsh words. I put my hands over my ears.

One man turned and beckoned me forward. His dark eyes seemed to hold kindness as well as fear, but I would not step toward him.

Finally they left, but they did not vanish. They pulled their small boat into the water and rowed back to the ship. I stood and watched, and some time later the small boat returned, with four men this time, at least three of them carrying muskets. They spoke in whispers as they rowed to shore and pulled the boat from the water. Again, the man with the kind eyes walked slowly toward me, beckoning. Three men stood behind him, guns loaded, ready to fire. They scanned the horizon all around them.

"Was it not a wondrous thing to see civilized men again?" Thevet rhapsodizes. "To hear men's words? It must have seemed like the angels had come again, like God had answered your prayers at last."

The voices mock: *Prayers. La bienveillance et la pitié de Dieu. Le silence.*

"Although I understand," he says, consternation displayed on his doughy face, "that it took some time for the men to persuade you to come with them." His laugh is incredulous. "They thought you did not want to leave that place."

The sun disappeared behind me and the sky darkened to wine. I turned and climbed toward the cave, still expecting the men and the ship to vanish. Instead the men followed me. I did not turn, but I could hear their footsteps behind me, scraping against rock. When we reached the entrance, a man holding a gun waved me aside and peered cautiously into the darkness. He entered the cave slowly.

A few moments later he emerged, chattering excitedly. *Un maouez!* he shouted. *Une femme! Elle est française!* This time I could understand a few French words mixed with his Breton. He gestured broadly as he described the trunk and then the citre. The men turned toward me, their faces even more fearful than if the man had declared me *une sauvage*. Three of them crouched low and went into the cave, but the man with the kind eyes stepped closer and tried to speak, his French halting.

Qui êtes-vous? he said. Who are you?

I was silent for a long time, listening to the chorus of *quork-quork-quork, pruk-pruk-pruk, cark-cark-cark* in the distance. Finally I said, *Le corbeau*, the raven.

His gaze shifted away, considered the open sea, then came back to me. Is there anyone else? he asked.

Non.

No others?

Only the dead.

Combien? How many?

I held up four fingers.

How long have you been here?

I waited. My throat hurt from the words scraping against tender flesh. I rubbed my neck and said, She was left in mid-summer, more than two years ago.

Who is *she*? Who are you?

When I did not answer, he held up two fingers. Two years?

Oui.

How did you get here?

Abandonnée.

Disbelief showed in his face and coloured his words. Abandoned? he asked. Who would have left you here?

The viceroy.

The viceroy of what?

New France. Roberval. The name was strange on my lips. The sound of it rose in the air and formed black smoke between us.

Two years? the man repeated. *Pourquoi?* Why?

"Why?" asks Thevet. "Why would you not want to leave that dreadful island?" The Franciscan's shrill voice hurts my ears. "Why?" he asks again.

"All that mattered was there."

His mouth pulls to one side. My answer seems to confound his simple mind.

The men looked at the darkening sky, then left the cave and returned to their small boat, which they rowed to the ship. I believed that was the end of it, that they and the ship would be gone in the morning.

That night I lay beneath the soft furs. I held the black feather and called him to me. He emerged from the fire's grey smoke. We loved. He stroked my cheeks and hair, sorrow in his mahogany eyes. And release.

I heard the voices then: *Fini. L'amour. Il est fini.* And knew he would not come to me again.

In the morning I selected a rock and made one more line on the smoke-darkened wall. Scrape of stone upon stone. Eight hundred and thirty-two.

When the men returned to the cave, they tried to take away the furs, Marguerite's trunk, and Michel's citre. I would not let them, though I could not stop them from taking the citre with its inlaid ivory and silver and copper.

I took only the iron pot, Michel's dagger, Marguerite's New Testament, and the ebony feather. I laid the pearl ring at the cave's entrance: a final gift for the ravens.

"But you did go," says the monk.

"I did."

Thevet looks at me as if he has solved a great puzzle. "And on the return voyage, you had weeks to plot."

"Plot?"

"Revenge."

"I cared nothing about revenge."

"But surely you wanted revenge against your uncle."

"My thoughts were upon all that I had left on the island."

"All you had left?" the Franciscan sputters. "Your trunk? Some old furs?"

Les corbeaux. Km-mm-mm. Les esprits. L'amour.

"Well, there would have been the remains of your lover and baby, I suppose." The monk lifts a chalice and takes a swallow of wine. He wipes the back of his hand across his mouth. "But surely you hated him, Marguerite. You must have sought him out."

"I never saw him again."

He points an accusing finger. "Ah, but you hired someone."

I reach within the folds of my skirt to run a thumb along the sharp blade of Michel's dagger. Perhaps I did. Or perhaps it was Lafrenière who hired the pockmarked man. Perhaps it was both of us – or neither – who paid him. Does it matter? Roberval is dead. And both of us are glad.

"The Queen of Navarre advised me to leave Roberval's fate in the hands of God," I say aloud. "And that is what I did."

Laughter: *Les mains de Dieu ou les mains des hommes? Km-mm-mm. Le meurtre ou la justice?*

"Justice," I murmur. Then, to the Franciscan, "You have never asked why Roberval killed her."

"Who?"

"Marguerite."

"This again," Thevet says wearily. "Obviously Roberval did not kill you, Marguerite. For here you are." He runs a finger around the rim of the chalice. "He was justified in punishing your scandalous behaviour. You were fortunate the viceroy did not toss you overboard to drown."

La justice ou le meurtre? Km-mm-mm.

I select my words carefully for the foolish monk. Can I explain to him, in a way he will understand, that Marguerite believed her uncle had money, that when I returned to France I discovered Roberval's wealth was a charade?

I cough to clear the pebbles from my throat. "Roberval had debts."

Thevet scoffs. "Many men, even nobles, have debts."

"He did not mean for Marguerite to marry anyone. Ever."

The monk shakes his head. "That cannot be true. If only someone suitable had asked for your hand…"

"Roberval had taken everything she had. He meant for her to die."

Thevet sucks in his cheeks. "I do not believe that."

My throat aches with the effort of speaking – and the futility. Never could I find the words to make Thevet understand that Roberval had planned everything, even before he left France. He did not abandon Marguerite because he was outraged at her behaviour. He abandoned her because he was deeply in debt. Her marriage would have required a dowry – and an accounting of her properties to her betrothed. Roberval had already spent Marguerite's small inheritance, already sold her family's *château*, even before the ships departed from France.

"You had him killed, didn't you?"

"I hope, *Père*, that I did. There would be some satisfaction in that."

He opens and closes his mouth, silently, like a beached fish.

I stand and smooth my black skirt. The pain in my throat has eased. "I have fulfilled my obligations to the king. We are done."

Still wrapped in a blanket, I rise from the bed and open the window to the morning light. I have slept long, without dreaming, and the sun is already well above the rooftops. The narrow beam admitted by the window illuminates the woodpile and the web, which now hangs in disrepair. The spider is gone, surfeited. I have fed her well. I have nothing more to give her.

I hear a timid knocking at the door, and hold my breath. It is Saint George's Feast Day. Surely he has not come again.

"Madame de Roberval." A small voice calling. Has she forgotten there is no school today?

I crack open the door. Isabelle holds up a bouquet of tiny blue flowers. "These are for you," she says.

Because I do not know what else to do, I open the door wider and take the flowers she offers. The slender stems are bruised, many of them broken. The blossoms are a pure sky blue, their centres like bright yellow suns. Forget-me-nots.

N'oubliez pas. Do not forget.

Before I can send her away, Isabelle walks boldly to the unmade bed and plops down, far more at ease than her father. "You must put them in water," she says with authority. "Or they will dry up." She looks around the room, her glance taking in the bench, the small table, the hearth, and the window.

"I am busy today, Isabelle. You must go."

"What will you do?"

"I will walk in the woods and fields." Why am I answering the questions of an impertinent child?

"May I come with you? I like to walk. Papa likes very much to walk. He says that he has his best thoughts when he is out in the woods." Isabelle squares her shoulders importantly and holds up a small silver coin. "Look what he gave me? He sent me to buy bread. All by myself." She giggles. "But he forgot the bakery is closed."

She stops her chatter only long enough to point toward the window. "Oh look," she says, "your cat." She rushes to the window and opens it wider. The yellow-striped cat backs away. "Here, kitty, kitty," she croons.

Slowly the cat creeps forward. Isabelle reaches out and touches her head. To my astonishment, the cat steps through the window.

"Do you have any cream?"

I shake my head.

"Have you anything?" Isabelle's voice is concerned. "I think she is very hungry."

As if in a dream I search for a bit of cheese and then hand it to Isabelle. She offers it to the cat, who sniffs, then gnaws hungrily. Isabelle runs her hand along the cat's back, and I think the cat will turn and scratch her. Instead she begins to purr.

"What's her name?" Isabelle asks.

I stand mute and blinking.

"She doesn't have a name?"

I shake my head.

"Oh, she must have a name." Isabelle puts a pudgy finger to her chin and stares upward, thinking hard and murmuring to herself. "Latin, I think." She proposes several names then dismisses them with a wave of her arm.

"I have it," she says excitedly. "*Laetitia.* Joy. That's perfect."

"*Laetitia,*" I whisper, somehow accepting that I now have a cat named Laetitia.

Être indulgent, c'est mourir. To be soft is to die.

I hear the voices, but I also hear Lafrenière: *to be soft is to be merciful...beneath your bitterness...*

Isabelle laughs. "Laetitia is skinny, but her tummy is fat." With her hands she draws a big belly in front of her own flat one. Her eyes widen with understanding. "Oh, may I have a kitten after they're born? Please," she pleads. "Papa will let me. I know he will."

Light-headed, I can only sit down and nod vaguely. Isabelle comes and takes my hand. Her fingers are warm and sticky. The cat follows her and rubs against her ankles.

Isabelle studies me closely. "Why are you always so sad?"

"Am I?"

"Very. Your face would be pretty...but it is always sad."

I pull my hand from Isabelle's and, inexplicably, reach to touch the cat. She allows me to stroke her fur. My fingers marvel at its matted softness. I can feel the rumbling purr through my fingertips. Tears gather. I cannot protect her and her kittens.

I hear an infant whimpering, the voices mocking: *La fille faible, la fille stupide. La fille naïve.*

"Is it because your husband and your baby died?"

I continue to stroke the cat and wonder if Isabelle too has heard the baby's hungry wails.

"Was he very handsome?"

"Very."

"I am sorry, Madame de Roberval."

"*Non, non,*" I say quickly. "It was not me. It was a different Madame de Roberval who lost her husband. I have lost no one."

Isabelle frowns and remains silent for a long time, stroking the cat. "I do that too," she confesses very quietly. "When I am very, very sad, I say to myself: 'Isabelle's mother was beautiful. She loved Isabelle. But she died. Poor Isabelle, she has no mother.'" She rubs the cat's cheeks. "Then I can feel sorry for Isabelle, and I don't feel so sad for me."

We sit for a while, petting the cat. "Papa says it's all right to do that," Isabelle whispers. The cat trills softly and rubs her side against my leg. I am startled at the silkiness and the warmth. Isabelle touches the cat's tattered ear. "How did that happen?"

"I do not know, Isabelle. I do not know who has hurt her."

Isabelle reaches up and wipes a single tear from my cheek. Her fingers smell of grass and flowers. The cat purrs, and we are quiet once more, petting and stroking, Isabelle's small hand bumping into mine.

"Was your baby very pretty?" she finally asks.

I sit for a long time, the pain in my throat choking me. "Her...my baby was beautiful." The words escape, sounding like hoarse croaks. "I did everything I could to save her. Everything."

Isabelle puts a hand to both sides of my face, her open palms like a benediction. "Of course you did," she says. "You loved her. You were her mother."

"*Oui*, I was her mother."

"I have learned of the poor unfortunate Damoiselle named Marguerite who was left by the Captain Roberval, her uncle, for the expiation of punishment for the scandal which she had made against the company which was voyaging to Newfoundland and Canada by the command of King Francis."

> André Thevet, *Grande insulaire,* unpublished manuscript,
> as translated by Elizabeth Boyer in *A Colony of One.*

"And she told me moreover that when they embarked on these Breton ships to return to France, that a certain desire seized her not to leave, and to die in that solitary place like her husband, her child, and her servant; and that she wished she were still there, moved by sorrow as she was."

> André Thevet, 1575, *Cosmographie universelle,*
> as translated by Roger Schlesinger and Arthur Stabler in
> *Andre Thevet's North America: A Sixteenth-Century View.*

"So living as to her body the life bestial, as to her soul the life angelical, she spent her time in reading of the Scriptures, in prayers and in meditations...The poor woman, seeing the ship draw near, went down to the strand, where she was when they came. And after praising God for it, she brought them to her hut...[T]hey took her with them to Rochelle...and made known to all that dwelt therein her faithfulness and patient long-suffering. And on this account she was received by all the ladies with great honour, and they with goodwill gave her their daughters that she might teach them to read and write. And in this honest craft she earned a livelihood, always exhorting all men to love our Lord and put their trust in Him, setting forth by way of example the great compassion He had shown towards her."

Marguerite d'Angoulême, Queen of Navarre, 1558,
The Heptameron, as translated by Arthur Machen in *The Heptameron: Tales and Novels of Marguerite Queen of Navarre.*

"Roberval had left them some food and other commodities to aid them and serve their necessity as he himself told me three months before he was killed at night near the Sainted Innocents in Paris since which time I have marked and given the name of Roberval to this island of banishment and also marked my maps for the great friendship that I bore to him while he lived."

André Thevet, *Grande insulaire*, unpublished manuscript,
as translated by Elizabeth Boyer in *A Colony of One.*

HISTORICAL NOTE

The historical documentation for the story of Marguerite de la Roque de Roberval is sketchy. Elizabeth Boyer, however, did extensive research to authenticate the documents surrounding the story and published her findings in *A Colony of One: The History of a Brave Woman* (Veritie Press: Novelty, Ohio, 1983).

Marguerite was an orphan, and Jean-François de la Roque de Roberval, a close male relative, became her guardian. It is likely that the Robervals were of the "new religion," known after the 1550s as the Huguenots.

In 1541 King François I appointed Roberval to be Viceroy of Canada and to colonize New France. Roberval's second-in-command, Jacques Cartier, left France for Canada in the spring of 1541. Roberval's departure was delayed for nearly a year, and his ships, the *Vallentyne*, *Sainte-Anne*, and *Lèchefraye* (sometimes listed as the *Marye*), left La Rochelle on April 16, 1542. Marguerite accompanied Roberval, along with 200 felons François I had released from French prisons specifically for the expedition.

Roberval's ships arrived in the St. John's harbour in Newfoundland on June 8, 1542, and remained there for several weeks. Jacques Cartier, having abandoned the colonizing efforts in Canada, met Roberval in St. John's and subsequently defied Roberval's order to return to Charlesbourg Royal, reportedly slipping away in the night to return to France.

Roberval's ships took a northern route from St. John's, passing through the Strait of Belle Isle into the Gulf of St. Lawrence. Somewhere along the way Roberval abandoned Marguerite, her lover, and a servant on the "Isle of Demons." The island has variously been identified as Fogo, Fichot, Quirpon, and Bell Island, all off the coast of Newfoundland, as well as Belle Isle in the Straits of Belle Isle. The most likely location for the Isle of Demons is Harrington Harbour, the largest of the Harrington Islands, along the lower north shore of Quebec about 220 km southwest of Blanc Sablon.

Roberval was known as a spendthrift, a man perpetually in debt, and also as a cruel man, but why he abandoned Marguerite, her lover, and the servant on a desolate island in a forbidding climate can be a matter only for conjecture.

Roberval's colony was a dismal failure. He and the surviving colonists returned to France in the spring of 1543, barely a year after leaving France. King François I then appointed Roberval minister of mines.

Marguerite, having lived for at least 27 months on the island, was rescued in the fall of 1544 by a Breton fishing ship. After she returned to France, she reportedly spent the rest of her life living near Angoulême and teaching young girls.

It is likely that Marguerite did tell her story to the Queen of Navarre, sister to François I and a sympathizer with the new religion. The queen retold Marguerite's story in her collection of tales, the *Heptameron*, which was published in 1558, after the queen's death. The queen disguised the characters' names and the details of the story.

The Franciscan André Thevet, cosmographer for four French kings and an antagonist to the Huguenots, interviewed Marguerite, reportedly in Nontron. Thevet retold her story in *La Cosmographie universelle d'André Thevet, cosmographe du roy*, published in 1575. Had he known the story earlier, he almost undoubtedly would have included it in his book, *Singularitez de la France antarctique,* published in 1557.

Thevet, who was known to his contemporaries as a liar and plagiarizer, wrote that Marguerite's lover died after eight months on the island, that Marguerite bore a child about a month later, and that Damienne, the servant, died about eight months after the child was born. The baby died about a month after Damienne. Thevet did not reveal either the name of the lover or the sex of the child.

Jean-François de la Roque de Roberval was reportedly murdered at the Church of the Innocents in Paris in the winter of 1560.

PRIMARY REFERENCES

Biggar, Henry P. *A Collection of Documents Relating to Jacques Cartier and the Sieur de Roberval.* Ottawa: Public Archives of Canada, 1930.

Boyer, Elizabeth. *A Colony of One: The History of a Brave Woman.* Novelty, Ohio: Veritie Press, 1983. (Can be obtained from: Women's Equity Action League, Elizabeth Boyer Books, P.O. Box 16397, Rock River, Ohio 44116 <Blissegan@cs.com>)

Garrisson, Janine. *A History of Sixteenth-Century France, 1484-1598: Renaissance, Reformation, and Rebellion.* New York: St. Martin's Press, 1995.

Heinrich, Bernd. *Mind of the Raven: Investigations and Adventures with Wolf-Birds.* New York: HarperCollins Publishers, 1999.

Johnson, Donald S. *Phantom Islands of the Atlantic.* Fredericton, NB: Goose Lane, 1994.

Johnson, Jean. "Marguerite de Roberval" in *Wilderness Women: Canada's Forgotten History.* St. John's: Centre for Newfoundland Studies, Memorial University, 1973.

The Holy Bible, Douay Rheims Version. 1609. Translated from the Latin Vulgate. Rockford, Illinois: Tan Books and Publishers, Inc., 1899.

King, Margaret L. *Women of the Renaissance.* Chicago: The University of Chicago Press, 1991.

Knecht, R. J. *The Rise and Fall of Renaissance France.* London: Fontana Press (HarperCollins), 1996.

Machen, Arthur. *The Heptameron: Tales and Novels of Marguerite Queen of Navarre.* New York: Alfred A. Knopf, Inc., 1924.

Lestringant, Frank. *Mapping the Renaissance World: The Geographical Imagination in the Age of Discovery.* Cambridge: Polity Press, 1994.

Ryan, D.W.S., Ed. *Legends of Newfoundland and Labrador.* St. John's: Jesperson Publishing Ltd., 1990.

Ryan, D.W.S., Ed. *The Legend of Marguerite: A Poem by George Martin.* St. John's: Jesperson Publishing Ltd., 1995.

Schlesinger, Roger and Arthur Stabler, Eds. *Andre Thevet's North America: A Sixteenth-Century View.* Kingston and Montreal: McGill-Queen's University Press, 1986.

Stabler, Arthur P. *The Legend of Marguerite de Roberval.* Seattle: Washington State University Press, 1972.

ACKNOWLEDGEMENTS

I am grateful to Amy Evans for her gracious and generous hospitality when I visited the Isle of Demons – Harrington Harbour – and I thank Christopher Lirette of Repentigny, Quebec, for taking the time to guide me to Marguerite's Cave. I also greatly appreciate Rhonda Molloy's immense talents in designing *Silence of Stone*.

Thanks also go to Patricia Casson-Henderson and Morgane Chollet for reviewing early drafts of the novel, and I am tremendously grateful and indebted to my daughters Amy and Megan Beckel Kratz and to Michele Bergstrom, Christine Champdoizeau, Debra Durchslag, Tom Joseph, Clyde Rose, Rebecca Rose, and Denise Wildcat for critiquing the penultimate draft of this novel. All of them gave me valuable comments worthy of serious consideration. My deepest appreciation goes to Pat Byrne who has supported and encouraged me since the very first word.

A novel of William Cormack's quest to save the Beothuk from extinction, his love for Shawnawdithit, a young Beothuk woman, and the tragedy of her life and the lives of her people. Based on historical and ethnographic accounts of the Beothuk, the novel is a fresh glimpse into a pivotal period of Newfoundland's heritage. Winner of the *Book Achievement Award for Best Fiction in 1999* from the Midwest Independent Publishers Association.

ISBN 1-55081-147-9 / $19.95 PB / 5 x 8 / 392 PP

"[A] major work…While the reader is ever conscious of the setting and the horrific tenor of the of the times…[Beckel] succeeds in breathing life into the characters; they are real and superbly individualized…a splendid literary creation that is an important socio-historical document as well…The pervasive darkness that this great novel depicts offers, too, the luminously redemptive influence of love. I have used the word 'great' in no facile way, I assure you, for the creation resonates with the power of the works of such masters as Hawthorne and Miller."

Enos Watts, author of *After the Locusts, Autumn Vengeance*, and *Spaces Between the Trees* (short-listed for the 2005 Winterset Award).

"[T]wo things make this book shine. First, the book is remarkably well researched. Beckel knows the period, from the pressures of religious wars that shook Germany down to details of city life, architecture and clothing…Secondly (and most rewarding for readers looking for more than a fresh account of the witch trials) is a series of small, bridging passages where the author allows Satan a first-person commentary on the ordeals that grip Eva."

Bruce Johnson, *Atlantic Books Today*.

"Sometimes there's an exceptional novel…Annamarie Beckel's *Dancing in the Palm of His Hand*…[is] a powerful, thought-provoking novel. Highly recommended."

Denise Moore, *Hi-Rise*.

"Ultimately, this is where Beckel's book shines: in its treatment of ordinary people faced with a disparity between their religious beliefs and their own moral sense."

Mark Callanan, *The Independent*.

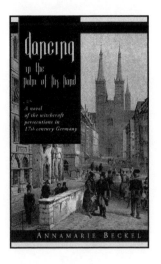

A novel about the horrors of the European witch persecutions as revealed through Eva Rosen, a young widow accused of witchcraft, her persecutor Wilhelm Hampelmann, and her defender Franz Lutz. A cautionary tale about the dangers of religious zealotry, the novel recreates the world of early 17th century Germany when sexual repression and religious war were rampant, rigid patriarchy prevailed in church, state, and family – and no one questioned the existence of witches or their master, the Devil.

ISBN 1-55081-217-3 / $19.95 PB / 5.5 x 8.5 / 320 PP

Annamarie Beckel at Marguerite's Cave, Harrington Harbour.
Photo by Christopher Lirette.

Annamarie Beckel lives in Kelligrews, Newfoundland. She first worked as an animal behaviourist and science writer, and then for fourteen years as a writer, photographer, and newsletter editor on the Lac du Flambeau Ojibwe reserve, before turning her research skills to historical fiction. *Silence of Stone* is her third novel.